Bad Penny

Bad Penny

Courter P. Donnelly

Peoh Point Press

Seattle, WA

Peoh Point Press

Seattle, WA. 98109

Print and electronic versions of Bad Penny by Courter P. Donnelly are available at amazon.com

Cover design by Greg Hollobaugh

ISBN: 9798392324484

For Barbara Finn of Fairfax, CA—at the center of a family of firefighters, long-time loving neighbor, all-around inspiration to the author, and recently named top borrower by the Fairfax Library.

Prologue

Sanctuary Lost

Paula freshens Red's water bowl as she makes the rounds, turning off lights and checking windows in the old cabin. Maneuvering in the dark, she feels her way along the hall and out onto the front porch. Hands finally at rest on the lacquered pine rail, she straightens her back, tops her lungs with night air, and stares into the black.

All the bedtime routines. Cut fluids. No iPhone after eight. Five milligrams of melatonin. And still she will not sleep past three.

The wind has risen, just as predicted by the weather service. Millions of pine needles rake the moving air, creating a sound like distant ocean surf. She concentrates on the shushing ebb and flow, pinpricks of Crest toothpaste and Bombay gin still registering on her tongue.

How many nights has she spent at her old cabin on the flank of Happy Mountain? Standing at this very spot.

A gust sends an empty garbage can tumbling. Still in soft slippers, she chases the escaped bin to the bottom of the driveway. There she steadies herself against the intensifying wind, the gentle shushing now a pounding surf. Suddenly, the motion-sensor floodlights above the garage door click on and illuminate the nearby stand of Ponderosa pines. As if a curtain has risen on a performance, the lights transform the churning trees into one of those bizarrely lit postmodern dances that Pete used to drag her to. Lots of violent thrashing with rooted feet, whipsawed backbones, and flailing limbs.

She closes her eyes against the memory. Time for bed, even if the sleep is over too soon.

*****

Around midnight, a lull in the windstorm registers in Paula's half-sleeping brain. She hears dried aspen leaves scrape across the driveway. A towhee issues a low, ratcheting tick-tick-tick. The windstorm has passed. Each cycle of deep breathing confirms it. But just as her thoughts begin to loosen and unspool into a dream, a powerful gust slams against the cabin and snaps Paula awake. She is upright in bed, her slim frame instantly drenched with adrenaline. Wooden joists moan and rock beneath her. Double-hung windows rattle as if uncaulked.

The howling over her cabin's roof is punctuated by pops and cracks from the walls. The red digits on her bedside clock have vanished, so Paula doesn't even try the lamp before putting on her sneakers and grabbing her phone and car keys. She only half-sees the reddish tint suffusing the bedroom and hallway.

She is feeling her way across the second floor landing when a second tsunami of wind hits the cabin. A window somewhere downstairs shatters. Her two-year-old granddaughter Brooklyn is standing in the doorway of her bedroom, dressed in her polar bear pajamas.

"Stay right there, Baby," Paula says. "I'm coming."

The wind mounts higher and higher in intensity and, as Paula bends to scoop up the girl, it detonates with a thunderous crack and a sickening crunch of timber. The whole cabin jumps and the front door blows wide open. Big Red shoots out from behind Brooklyn, gallops down the stairs and out of the door into the dark. Or actually, as Paula now realizes, into the odd reddish glow that fills the doorway and pulses at the window blinds. A fire truck already. How could that be?

Brooklyn in her arms, Paula flies down the stairs and through the buckled doorframe into the front yard. It must be safer outside than in the collapsing house, she thinks, but the wind instantly shoves her sideways and propels her into a crazy stagger, her shuffling steps the only thing that prevents her from toppling over or dropping the child. She steadies herself, back against the wind, feet planted wide, nightgown billowing like a parachute between her legs, and squeezes the girl to her chest. The hot wind, dense with grit and pine needles, rolls over her hunched body.

A pine branch bashes the side of her head, the needles strafing her eyes. Brooklyn wails. Oh for fuck's sake, Paula thinks, maybe it is safer inside. She turns and stumbles over a quart-sized yogurt carton that's rolling at high speed toward the garage. Her eyes follow the container as she tries to make sense of the landscape in front of her. The massive Ponderosa pine where her seed feeders hang has slammed through the new garage addition and its adjoining study, slicing all the way to the concrete pad. The metallic tang of just-split wood fills the air.

She holds Brooklyn tight against buffets of hot air and looks north to the ridge. A wall of wine-colored smoke billows above the horizon. Burgundy light illuminates the whole surreal scene: the downed tree, the crushed garage, and now the week's recycling caught in a crazy whirlpool churning across the front yard.

"Okay, Baby," she says into her granddaughter's ear, finally making a move for the cabin. The door is stuck open, the frame probably knocked out of true, but the house looks stable. "This is a big wind, isn't it? We'll be okay. Let's keep an eye out for Big Red. You wait right here for him." She carefully places Brooklyn under the oak dining table, a relic of her own childhood. "Stay right there on your knees, Baby."

When Paula heard about the Red Flag Warning early that morning, she double-checked thc plastic emergency bins in the garage. Water, dried and canned food, dog food, radio, flashlights, batteries, the old camp cook kit with fuel, medical stuff. All set to go, next to the car. Like always. She'd written enough sad stories about fires and earthquakes to know more than most about preparedness. About preparedness and stupidity and fate.

But now the Honda was likely crushed in the garage. And it might not be safe to get the supplies.

Paula hurries back to the porch, halfway believing she's still dreaming. But the garage is truly crushed, and embers fill the air. The red pixels touch down in sprinkles and waves. A tiny nebula explodes at Paula's feet, skitters past her legs, and races across the tiled entry into the house. The roar from the north sounds like a blowtorch. She can barely stand, much less think straight. The smell of smoke reaches her nose.

Only one idea sticks: the International Harvester truck behind the house. The '74 crew cab. Her father's pride and joy. Not started in months. She turns once more and looks out beyond the front yard.

"Red," she yells into the gale, cupping her hands around her mouth. "C'mon, Red boy!"

Smoking briquettes plunk from the sky. The red sparks still rush aloft in loops and spirals, but these heavier grey chunks rain down with more purpose, at consistent angles, bouncing and rolling and settling on the lawn like a barrage of scorched golf balls.

Just before the smoke blots out everything, Paula spots the first tall tongues of flame on the ridge.

"Brookie," she yells, turning toward the door, "we've got to go now. Come on, Baby."

*****

The cabin on Happy Mountain is five miles from the paved road leading to the town of La Likt. As soon as Paula turns onto the forest road and points the old truck's headlights downhill, she feels protected from the sparks and embers and the wind's body blows.

They stop near the gate at the bottom of the drive to call once more for Red, and Paula honks the old truck's fading horn. The smoke and the deafening roar of the wind, she knows, make the efforts futile. They move on. Twice she stops to drag a fallen branch off the road. After the second stop, Brooklyn shifts in her car seat.

"Gramma, where Red? Where Big Red?" she asks, her first utterance all night. Paula worries sometimes about the girl's silence.

"The big animals can run," she says, reaching back, taking the child's hand, and squeezing gently. "Red will hide tonight," she says in a sing-song voice. "He'll come back tomorrow. We have to go now."

For almost a year now she's been her granddaughter's legal guardian. Brooklyn's daddy and mommy—her son, his girlfriend— were struggling with addiction, or, more precisely, living in a tarp-covered tent off Aurora Avenue in Seattle. Through all the bad days —Pete's illness and death, their son's addiction, the stress of caring for a child again in her sixties—Red, Pete's Hungarian Vizsla, was a solitary note of joy.

Well. Red and Brooklyn.

Just a mile down the hill, Paula slows at the side road leading to Cassie Wojciechowski's ranch. The metal gate hangs wide open. Did Cassie get the animals out? Smoke obscures Paula's view of the house.

Brooklyn follows her grandmother's gaze up the road. "Red and Mommy go with Cassie and Holly," she states as if it's simply a well-known fact. Rather than a secret. Or a crime.

Paula looks in her rearview mirror and sees only the blonde top of Brooklyn's head. Above her granddaughter, filling the tiny rectangular rear window, a micro-current of sparks tumbles over the back of the cab.

"I know he does, Baby," Paula replies, ready to roll ahead, hand already on the stick shift—until a movement on the road toward the ranch house catches her eye.

Before she can think, Paula swings the old truck through Cassie's gate, scattering gravel between the pines. Her windshield wipers swat at a scrim of ash.

"We'll just take a quick look for Red," Paula says, more to herself than to Brooklyn.

"Here we go," she says, thumping the steering wheel as they penetrate the cluster of trees near the ranch's upper pasture. "Let's go get Big Red, Baby."

Big Red, litter mate of Penny.

Big Red, who was not big.

Part 1: The Happy Mountain Fire

Chapter 1

Beth has a shock

I stood just inside the door of the La Likt Senior Center, next to the table where the sign-in sheet and sticky-backed name tags sat untouched, and scanned the crowd at the Happy Mountain fire community meeting for a glimpse of my husband. At one point I thought I caught sight of his slim frame slicing through the crowd and I blundered off in pursuit. I went so far as to grab on to my quarry's arm before I realized my error.

"Oops, sorry!" I sputtered when the man, Nathan-like but not Nathan, turned and gazed down at me. His spooky grey eyes immediately emptied of curiosity once he got a good look—white woman in late middle age, blonde bob going gray, wearing the oversized, black-framed reading glasses that were in style five years ago and a T-shirt that would have been white if it hadn't got mixed up with a dark load of laundry. I lifted my hand off his arm so quickly that my elbow caught the woman behind me square in her pillowy chest, and by the time I finished apologizing to her Nathan's double had moved on. Now he was standing with the new guy in town, the one we call The Italian because, well, he's Italian.

Somewhere in his twenties, with perfectly tousled black curls and immaculate footwear. Always walking. No car. Not a lot of English.

I finally found my husband hovering near the table that held free cookies and coffee. He was alternately taking bites out of a huge, paste-white grocery store snickerdoodle and talking to the editor of the North Sahaptin County Courier, our weekly newspaper and, more recently, the county's source for local news online.

"But it's not all bad, Jim," Nathan was saying. "Fire has an important place in our environment. Take woodpeckers. Woodpeckers love burned trees. Woodpeckers need burned trees."

"Maybe they do, Nathan, but you're going to have a hard time winning over the folks on La Likt Ridge," Jim replied. "They're looking at losing their homes. Woodpeckers don't really fit into their concerns right now."

I tugged at my husband's flannel sleeve. "You're not going to write about the woodpeckers, are you?" I asked, though I admit it may have sounded more like a warning than a question.

"Beth!" Nathan responded cheerily. He removed his sweat-stained Mariners baseball cap, absently raked an overgrown thatch of salt-and-pepper hair back from his forehead, and clamped the hat back down again as if that would set the world aright. His fingernails were filthy. "I'm already writing about how important wildfires are for woodpeckers in The Straight Poop and I thought maybe Jim would want to pick up the column on his new website."

I struggled to contain my exasperation. After all, we were in public, and in a small town like La Likt you have to be careful about what people see. I've learned that the hard way.

"But Nathan," I said, "The Straight Poop is for supporters of High Country Crapper, and those people are already on board with," I paused, searching for the right words. "Certain unpopular ideas," I concluded.

High Country Crapper is my husband's nonprofit organization and one true love. Officially, it's the Drake Water Quality Project, but since the org's main work is installing and maintaining outhouses in environmentally sensitive wilderness locations, most people prefer the common name. Nathan's passion for poo has made him a bit of a local celebrity. Also, a bit of an oddball—a city-bred water quality specialist who once worked for the government now living in a town where almost everybody's grandaddy worked for the Patrick coal mines (closed, 1964), the railroad (bankrupt, 1972), or the logging companies (reduced to salvaging logs after wildfires, present day).

"But that's exactly why I want to write about woodpeckers in the Courier," Nathan said. "Get the message out to a bigger audience—"

A high-pitched, electronic hum cut him off. At the front of the room, a burly man wearing Forest Service green held a dainty, corded microphone between right thumb and forefinger. Next to him, a guy dressed in the dark blue of our county fire department fiddled with the keyboard of a laptop.

"Good evening, everyone. If we could get you all to sit down, we're about to start," the Forest Service rep said. "Those of you standing in the back, we've got lots of seats up front here."

Jim, Nathan, and I slipped into the front row next to Cassie Chimpanzee, the woman who runs the sanctuary for former research apes on the eastern outskirts of town. Her real name is Cassie Wojciechowski, but useful nicknames seem to stick around here. Right now, Cassie's chimps were in their trailer out in the parking lot. If their home was gone, it wouldn't be easy to find another one.

"So, some seats left up here," the Forest Service rep repeated, pointing to spaces on either side of us. The crowd in the back declined the offer with a disgruntled murmur.

"Okay. I'm Incident Commander Russell Hinges," the burly man said. "Some people call me Rusty."

He paused a moment to let us sound that out in our heads.

"I'm joined here tonight by representatives of the Department of Natural Resources, Sahaptin County Emergency Services, the Sheriff's Department, and your local fire officials to update you on the Happy Mountain fire." A slide popped up on the screen behind him, a checkerboard map of the land about 25 miles upriver from town. A dark red border marked off a good portion of La Likt Ridge.

"The Happy Mountain incident started August 13 over on the north side of the ranger district," Rusty Hinges said, jabbing at the screen with a steel pointer. "Remember we had a storm come up that night—wind gusts 80 miles an hour over the ridges—and that spread fire quickly downslope here"—more pointing—"and up over Happy Mountain toward the housing developments at the base of La Likt Ridge and the towns of Patrick and La Likt. This necessitated both voluntary and mandatory evacuation orders for many of you." Hinges let the pointer fall to his side and drew a breath. "Now the good news," he began.

"How many of our houses are gone?" yelled a man in the back. He had a robust baritone and the question seemed to ring from the stainless-steel roll-ups that wall off the senior center's kitchen.

"Getting to that," said Hinges, "but the good news is we had a lucky break with the weather. Humidity increased, wind shifted, and the fire has slowed significantly here in section E, closest to the towns." The fire official at the laptop zoomed the map to section E.

"Now," said Hinges. "Our first priority is safety, for our crews and all of you who live here. Our second priority is to protect assets in the path of the fire. We've got 260 personnel on the ground, and our dozer and hand crews are working hard."

"How many structures are gone," the man in back demanded. "Who's burning down our homes?"

While those on either side of him roared their encouragement, I wrenched myself around to get a look at the speaker. He was a lean, well-groomed old guy, maybe 75, in tan Lee Wranglers that looked like the cowboy cut to me. He topped off the Wranglers with a snap button shirt and a bolo tie, the strings held together by an impressive piece of polished Ellensburg blue agate. In other words, the full ranching package, including a Stetson to park on his full head of white hair.

"Who's that?" I whispered.

"Roger Thorp," Cassie whispered back. "Lower county asshole. Not sure what business he has up here."

"So, we'll take questions when we get through the summary," said Hinges. Somebody booed loudly. Another yelled, "This is our country and we've got a right to know!"

"We're at 27 percent containment and we expect to increase that number relatively quickly," said Hinges.

"We don't care about percentages, we care about our homes!" Thorp boomed. "Who's burning them down?"

"Unfortunately, we have had structure loss," Hinges said. Another slide appeared on the screen, a drone shot with individual building sites outlined in red and green. "We've still got to get assessment teams in, but we know the La Likt Ridge Townhomes have been severely impacted. And while firefighters saved several single-family residences in the affected zone, our initial count shows 11 outbuildings lost." He took in a fortifying breath. "And a dozen or so residences."

A few people in the crowd cried out—sharp, involuntary sounds as if a stranger had stepped up and given them a hard slap. "Goddamn arsonist!" one of Thorp's gang yelled. "Time to take him out!" The group around him roared their approval.

"Whoa, whoa, whoa!" Our local fire official jumped up from behind his laptop and stood next to Rusty Hinges, hands up, palms out. "Most of you know me. Jaylen Hoyt, district six fire chief. Now, Roger and all you back there, we all know there's been several small fires around town this summer. In the community forest over next to

Patrick. That dumpster behind Dave's tavern. The one out by the lake campground. Nobody's lost much of anything—you know that—but we've had close calls."

An ominous grumbling came from the back of the room.

"We're investigating these fires and, if any look like arson," Hoyt paused and raised his voice, "which we don't know if it is arson, but if it looks that way, we're going to get some help from the State investigators."

"State investigators," Thorp spat the words out like they tasted of kerosene and lead. "We already know somebody's setting the fires. How're the jumbucks from Olympia going to stop that?"

"Shut up and let Jaylen talk," a woman mid-crowd responded. I was relieved to hear several people around her voice their agreement. At least the whole town hadn't yet been driven nuts by fire season and their social media feeds.

"Thank you," Hoyt said, nodding at the group seated in front of him, which included us. I squirmed a little, feeling eyes on the back of my head. "Now, this fire, the Happy Mountain incident. It's orders of magnitude larger than what we've been seeing close in town. And, Rusty, I know you plan to go over this later, but preliminary findings are this one started with a lightning strike over by Icicle."

The noise level in the lunchroom increased, with some people cursing and others telling them to pipe down and everyone else generally looking for someone to blame for fire coming into their lives. Likely it was some camper letting their toasted marshmallows get out of hand. Or the government fools who watch the land catch and then just sit back while it burns. Maybe, I worried, people suspected it was a woodpecker lover who thinks it's good news when the forest goes up in flames. I twisted nervously in my seat to get another look at the back row and noticed a whole crew of camouflage-clad guys bobbing around just behind Thorp's Stetson.

The men at the front of the room, their meeting highjacked, switched off the slide deck and tried to restore order.

"We're going to break up into groups," Hinges yelled through his tiny microphone. "We're going to have agency reps in each corner of the room, and you can come up to us and ask questions. Civilly, folks, please."

Cassie was out of her folding chair before Hinges could escape to his corner.

"Rusty," she said, grabbing his arm. "Has anyone seen my neighbor Paula Novak, from up off Happy Mountain Road? Her and her little granddaughter Brooklyn? I haven't been able to find them."

*****

People stood in worried knots, trying to figure out when they might be able to go home or if they had a home to go to, as Nathan, Cassie, and I left the meeting and walked into the smoky evening. The sun, a fuzzy orange disc, was sinking through the mucky gray sky to the west, casting the senior center parking lot in a reddish glow that reminded me of the latest pictures from Mars. The air, now an acrid fog, smelled like a fully booked campground on Labor Day weekend. I coughed, and Nathan rubbed my back. "It's going to get worse," he said quietly. "We'll probably get ash fall from this one."

Nathan and I had been lucky so far this fire season. Our little log cabin, which we'd been trying to bring up to code for the past two summers, was located far enough down valley to be out of the official mandatory evacuation zone. Cassie, though, had endured a harrowing night when the Happy Mountain fire swept over La Likt Ridge. She'd stuffed her feet into the boots she kept ready by her bed and run out into the swirling darkness. The ridge glowed orange and swarms of yellow-red sparks flew across the pastureland that made up the chimp sanctuary.

"Like videos of a war, you know?" she told us. "Tracer fire?"

Cassie and her chimps had practiced evacuation before, but the real thing was much harder. For one thing, Cassie was alone, and it wasn't easy to singlehandedly wrangle seven fully grown chimps, each of whom had his or her own ideas about the situation.

"I always thought I'd have some warning before fire evacuation," she told us. "As soon as we got word of any kind of fire, Paula was supposed to come down the hill and help me get the chimps out."

Cassie looked down at her dirty hands, then clasped them together and squeezed until the knuckles showed white. "But it wasn't like that," she said. "I woke up and the fire was already on us. I had to get them loaded quick. Didn't even have time to get our emergency packs, so we'll just have to make do with the supplies in the trailer."

She looked toward the hills behind the senior center, where a swelling cloud of smoke—a cross between an enormous thunderhead and Armageddon—hung over the fire. The west wind, a permanent presence in our town due to luckless placement of a gap in the mountains, caught hold of the senior center's door just as a family tried to leave. We watched the father struggle against the wind-caught plate glass while his wife and two kids made for the safety of the family truck.

"You know Holly, my lead chimp," Cassie said in a choked whisper. "She ran off. I opened all the gates for her, but I had to leave her behind."

"We'll get her," Nathan said, likely with more certainty than he felt. "As soon as we can, Cassie. We'll go back up to your place and find her. She's probably hunkered down somewhere on the property."

"And you can keep the chimps at our place for now," I said, surprising myself as well as Nathan, who took a quick step away from me like he might finally make a break from our 29 years of marriage. I figured we could put the chimps up in Penny's run—Penny's our dog—at least until the county made us move them.

Cassie sighed like she'd been holding her breath for a week. "Thanks, Beth. That's a real relief. And Nathan," she said, turning toward my husband, "I would like to get up to the place as soon as we can. Rusty Gates or whoever back there," she tilted her head toward the senior center, "he said property owners would probably be able to get an escort in tomorrow."

One of the trailered chimps hooted, which started the whole group whooping like GenXers at a Pearl Jam concert. Cassie took in a long breath. "Plus, you know, it's not just Holly. Nobody's seen Paula and Brooklyn since the day before yesterday."

I felt my stomach drop. Paula Novak was one of the few friends I had in La Likt, probably because we'd met in Seattle. When I joined the staff of the city's newspaper more than 20 years ago, she was my editor, and we'd worked closely together until her retirement. I was amazed, and, I'm embarrassed to say, more than a little dismissive, when she left the ultra-progressive city for the few acres of parched hillside she owned outside of La Likt, population 2,000 and all but the babies flag-waving members of the Eagles Club.

In my defense, it would be hard to find two places more perfectly opposed than Paula's old city and her new town. Seattle sat perpetually damp in the spot where rainstorms swept around the Olympic Mountain range, blew over the Puget Sound, and stalled against the barrier of the Cascade Mountain range. La Likt was dry and deep in the rain shadow, 30 miles on the other side of the main east-west pass and split by six lanes of interstate highway. Seattle was young, international, and wealthy, with a workforce drawn by an ever-changing list of companies about to become household names. La Likt was like your uncle who never left home: aging, set in his ways, and not quite able to get by on his own.

Once we'd visited Paula a few times, even Nathan and I saw the charms of La Likt—the way migrating yellow warblers lit up the willow branches in spring and the dance of dry grass in the wake of the freight trains on long summer evenings. In the winter, a week of snow and rain would often be followed by skies as clear as California. Plus, you could always find parking in front of wherever you wanted to be in La Likt and the plastic bags at the grocery store came free of charge. Right before we quit our day jobs, Nathan and I bought our 120-year-old miner's cabin on the south side of the interstate with plans to renovate it for our own retirement. For now, we still held on to our west-side townhome in Seattle. But I wondered how long that would last.

After all, what tied us to the city? Since Nathan sold the patent for his slick little water filter and we got enough money to retire a little earlier than planned, what tied us anywhere? My mom died almost two years ago, my brothers were both on the East Coast, and my sister—well. None of us is sure where she is. Nathan's dad lived comfortably close to his pew-load of siblings in Sacramento. Our current responsibilities ended with Penny, and all she seemed to require was a daily walk and her fuzzy blanket.

The three of us were independent, I liked to remind Nathan. Not to say unmoored.

So far, making friends among the first families of La Likt was not coming easily to a me, which is one reason I like knowing that Paula is nearby. I like to think she appreciates my presence too, especially since she's become Brooklyn's guardian. The streets aren't a good place to raise a child, especially if you have to spend a lot of time finding your next dose. That's what Paula says, and it's why she went to court to get Brooklyn's guardianship. After a particularly trying couple of months during which Brooklyn and her parents tried living with Paula in La Likt, she even tried to convince James and Chloe to abandon their parental rights. After that, relations between Paula and her son became even more strained.

To be fair, it's not like Brooklyn's mom and dad haven't made efforts. Twice, with Paula's help, they've gone to rehab. And twice they've been pulled back in. The last time I talked to Paula, she told me James had managed to get into another program—this time without his mother's help. When I told her I thought that was good news, Paula said she was done feeling hopeful, and I thought of the sad day she'd told me she'd filed for a restraining order against her son—the only family she had left. In my mind, James was still the tow-headed six-year-old who hung around the newsroom with Paula on rainy Saturdays 20 years ago. I wondered now who would let him know that both his mother and his daughter were missing.

*****

The next morning Nathan, Cassie, and I joined a caravan of vehicles headed up the crumbling road toward the chimp sanctuary. It was a sorry, anxious procession. Red-eyed women wearing borrowed sweatpants and charcoal-smudged tank tops. Grim men squeezing the steering wheels of ashy half-ton pickups. The few kids who hadn't been dropped off with family or friends were hanging close to their parents, wide-eyed and silent.

Cassie, Nathan, and I definitely were the outliers: the chimp lady accompanied by the High Country Crapper dude and his weirdo wife. We'd all managed to stand out in town before, and not usually in a good way. You don't necessarily want people noticing you bellowing along to your favorite Katy Perry playlist while a bunch of chimps hoot the chorus (Cassie), or slinking around the transfer station, slowly reloading your Subaru with items you'd planned to dump (Nathan), or clanking through the Safeway with every last bottle from a rogue shipment of Sancerre in your cart (guess who). People in a small town remember these things.

The trucks peeled off one by one and headed up dirt driveways to homes behind metal ranch fences now twisted by the intense heat of the fire. It looked like most of the houses had been saved by the firefighters—islands of normality amid blackened pines and scorched pastureland. But we knew some places had been lost. When it came time for us to separate from the caravan, I couldn't help squeezing my eyes shut.

Cassie wheeled her truck through the main gate into her yard and shut off the engine. "Well," she said slowly, "first glance, could be worse."

My eyes popped open, and from the cab of the truck I could see that Cassie's ranch house still stood. The chimp house was there, too, but the windows were blown out and black scorch marks climbed up the cinder block walls. I couldn't tell about Cassie's shed, which was too far up the drive to see, but aside from a couple of gnarled specimens in what used to be an apple orchard, the trees around her place were all dark trunks and singed needles.

I got out of the cab to join Nathan on the driveway. Cassie was already inside her house.

"It's a miracle, but it looks good in here," she said when she bustled out of the front door a few minutes later. "I mean, there's smoke damage and some puddles, but all things considered, it's good. Come on, let's find Holly before the escort comes back for us."

"I'll check out the upper pasture," Nathan said, starting for the field above us.

Cassie and I made our way up the paved drive to the chimp house. The scene wasn't as happy here. Fire had made its way inside and consumed the chimps' bedding, toys, and supplies. The concrete structure still looked sound, though we found no sign of Holly.

"Probably can reboot the chimp house," Cassie said as we rounded the bend in her drive and got our first look at the place her storage building should be. "But it looks like the shed is gone. And no Holly."

"Cassie," Nathan called down to us, "did you have another old truck here?" He was pointing toward a gravel road that snaked into some trees at the edge of the upper pasture. "Looks like an International Harvester?"

"I don't have an IH," Cassie said. "But Paula does." She took off at a run up the gravel road and I sprinted after her.

The truck, its color made indistinguishable by a thick layer of ash and dust, was trapped in the middle of the road. The fire seemed to have hopscotched over it, but the trunk of a middling-sized pine lay across its stove-in cab.

"Paula!" I screamed in a high, ragged voice I hardly recognized. "My God, are you in there?"

She was, crushed and still against the truck's steering wheel, blood dark in her gray hair and on her bare knees below her cotton nightgown. Hooked on the bench seat behind her was a child's car seat, empty, with the restraining straps unbuckled.

Chapter 2

Nathan looks for likes

I sat at our battered kitchen table, looking for the right words. They needed to acknowledge the mood of the community but also to get across the deeper significance of this scary moment. All while catering to local sensibilities. It was a tricky balance. Finally, I typed:

[DRAFT BLOG POST #18]
The Straight Poop
OFFICIAL BLOG OF THE DRAKE WATER QUALITY PROJECT

The Fire in Context

Emotions were understandably high at the Happy Mountain fire community meeting. At least 12 homes were destroyed and, hard to fathom, we also lost Paula Novak, a true pillar of the Upper Sahaptin community. A former Seattle journalist who had lived in her family's Happy Mountain cabin for more than a decade, Paula contributed her boundless energy to many of our community's leading environmental and social organizations. She was a close friend of our family and a generous contributor to the Drake Water Quality Project.

Perhaps even more difficult to comprehend, Paula's granddaughter Brooklyn still has not been found. Even as hotspots remain, brave fire specialists continue to search the area around the Novak cabin and Cassie Wojciechowski's adjoining chimp sanctuary.

At this time, thankfully, we are unaware of any losses to DWQP facilities or equipment in the Happy Mountain region.

So, yes, voices were raised at the community meeting. Hard questions DO need to be asked about how the fire started—was it related to other recent smaller fires on the fringes of La Likt?—and why it could not be controlled.

But at some point, and I realize it may be too early for this discussion, we as a community also need to understand and address the larger context in which these wildfires are burning. Two points are critical.

1. The fires we see today are in large measure due to a century of fire suppression. The dog-hair pines our hunters and hikers now encounter on the east Cascade slopes are the post-logging legacy of Forest Service policy—our nation's policy—until just recently. Without the natural burns caused by lightning or by indigenous peoples the forests became overgrown. [WEAVE IN MENTION OF CLIMATE CHANGE? MAYBE NOT.] Only newer forest management practices, including prescribed burns and small-diameter logging, will lead us back to any semblance of forest health. When appropriate, away from homes, a let-it-burn containment policy may also be needed.

2. Fire is a dynamic part of our forest ecology. [FIND ANOTHER WORD FOR 'ECOLOGY'?] Not only have

we lost the mature signature trees of our east-slope biogeography—the old-growth Ponderosa pines, the open meadows of the subalpine belt—we have also squeezed out the native fauna associated with those special lands as well as the specialists who depend on fire to make their living. The black-backed woodpecker (Picoides arcticus), for example, absolutely depends on fires to create suitable habitat. Also known as the three-toed woodpecker, this elegant fellow with splotchy white underside and (in the male) a yellow cap, feeds on the wood-boring beetles found only on recently burnt trees. The excitement of spotting a three-toed in a burn zone is unmatched and... [ETC. NEEDS MORE DETAIL. FOCUS ON NEW STUDIES OF WOODPECKER RANGE IN THE TIETON REGION? PERHAPS ADD A WHOLE SEPARATE BLOG POST IN FUTURE?]

As our community absorbs the loss [BLAH BLAH, WRAP UP AND CALL TO ACTION...]

The blog post still needed work. The ending. More detail on the beautiful and rare three-toed woodpecker. Tweaks to avoid hot-button words. But the howling chimps in my garage made it difficult to concentrate.

I pushed away from the table. "When did rural folk become so trigger happy over any word hinting of science?" I asked Beth, trying for a light-hearted tone.

"You should cut by half," she replied on her way into the bedroom with an armful of clean sheets. "Ask yourself, 'What am I trying to say?' Then just say it."

Had she even seen the draft yet? I think not. But she knew better than anyone my tendency to ramble on about certain topics. Like wilderness privies. Birds. Geology. Evolution. Lots of things, actually. Especially when the magical internet placed no theoretical bounds on word count. And when I, Nathan Drake, was editor and sole commander of my own nonprofit's blog.

She was probably right.

"You still trying to get in touch with James Novak?" I asked.

"Yeah, but he's on the streets again," she answered. "There's still a restraining order against him and Chloe, and it includes Brooklyn. Might be tricky." She sounded exhausted.

"I can ask Bill Chaney about that," I offered. Bill was our neighbor in La Likt as well as our go-to attorney for matters of real estate, estate planning, and taxes. And now, I guess, questions involving the rights of drug-addicted parents to search for their daughter who has gone missing in a wildfire.

Beth stood, looking confused about why her phone was suddenly in her hand. "Yeah, no," she said. "Maybe." Then she went into the bedroom and closed the door to make more calls.

I tried to return to my writing, but I couldn't concentrate. It's like the damned chimps were being tortured out there in our almost-finished, soon-to-be-magnificent garage. Also, I was still amped up by the fire. Beth and I had hardly slept since we found Paula. How was Beth ever going to get over the loss of one of her best friends? Being Paula's executor and responsible for contacting family and friends probably wasn't helping.

I was worried about Beth. I suppose there's never a good time for the grief that descends with the untimely death of a good friend. But Beth was still only a few years out from the loss of her mother. And she would always carry the burden related to the unresolved disappearance of her big sister Laura when Beth was just a third grader. Kidnap? Runaway? Murder? That was an open-ended grief that aged and took on new shapes, but did not lessen.

I tried to be supportive, but also to give Beth her space. At present, she seemed intent on carrying out her role as Paula's executor. Who knows? Having a defined role might be a good thing, a distraction with actual meaning and value. Penny, too, it occurred to me, might be a good thing for her right now. A copper-coated comfort.

We found Penny, our Hungarian Vizsla, wandering the trails above a puppy mill set up in a broken-down ranch house on the fringes of the wilderness. Now she was a constant presence in our lives, joining us on most of our walks and traveling back and forth with us from our work-in-progress cabin here in La Likt to our townhouse in Seattle. It was hard to remember life before her.

But where was our floppy-eared Penny now? I glanced around me. She was not curled up in the corner of the living room, her usual spot when I was pecking away at my laptop. I didn't see her out in her pen either. That had been busted up for months and was still awaiting repair with back-ordered six-gauge wire panels.

Most likely the nonstop shrieking of my cousins out in the garage had driven Penny away from the house.

Good thinking, Penny. I slid my laptop into my daypack and headed for my friend Dave's brew pub, the Cenozoic, where I could edit my blog post in peace. Then maybe I'd pick up some fresh salmon and corn for a simple grilled dinner. Beth needed a relaxing night and some sleep. My goal was to provide support services, for the most part, and to stay out of the way to let Beth come to terms with her new sorrow.

My footsteps crunching on the gravel of our drive roused the half dozen chimps to new levels of grievance. Cassie had given us a quick lesson on how to feed, water, and clean up after the caged chimps, but frankly I was not comfortable around our temporary guests. Apparently I was not as evolved as I thought. After all, Darwin first saw chimps and orangutans at the London Zoo in 1838 and we all know how that turned out. I, however, seemed to share the uneasy fascination felt by Queen Victoria after her visit to the same zoo exhibition. As I recall she called them "frightful, painfully and disagreeably human." No wonder I felt watched and judged every time I entered our big garage. And really, why wouldn't those poor animals see me as their jailer and torturer? Who could blame them for the ruckus.

As I reached the Subaru, I saw our neighbor Kathy Chaney, Bill the attorney's wife, striding down the street toward me, and it looked like she had Penny. Kathy was a stout woman usually dressed in a colorful outfit. Today, it was white sneakers, tan jeans, and a red fleece shirt partially covered with her trademark turquoise down vest. Penny's head hung down as if she was ashamed to be seen on the short purple leash normally tugged by Kathy's dog, Roxy the Chihuahua.

"Nathan," Kathy called, a red arm up. "A word?"

"Hey Kathy," I said, waiting in the street. When she finally stood in front of me, I wasn't sure how to start the conversation. Kathy wasn't letting Penny off the leash, as I expected, and Penny was still staring dejectedly at the pavement, her long silky ears actually touching the ground.

Kathy also seemed to be confused about what to say. Then, as she drew a deep breath and looked down at my dog, it became clear that the normally placid Kathy Chaney was struggling to temper some kind of real anger against our years of friendship.

"Kathy," I asked with mounting anxiety, "what's going on?"

She tugged on the leash. Penny finally met Kathy's cold stare then slowly lowered her rear to one of those hovering just-barely sits.

"Penny needs some training, Nathan," Kathy began, her accusing eyes now swinging around to me. "She's been coming up and harassing our chickens. She's always been a little frisky with Roxy, and that's okay I guess, but now she's digging around the coop. And today she got hold of Mr. Clucker. I saw it."

She gulped and clucked a bit herself. "Out the window, I saw it. She had him—" Here Kathy's nerve failed her, and she let her voice fade into heavy sniffling. "I barely got there in time," she managed.

I was stunned silent. Penny was such a sweet and loving dog. She had responded to our care and close attention by blossoming into a curious and friendly little hound who loved to walk everywhere with us and responded to our every command. Indeed, she seemed to anticipate our desires and deliver with the purest of hearts. She had eyes only for me and Beth.

Now I looked down at Penny and made the clicking sound with my tongue that had always been our special signal. She gave me just a glance before rolling her eyes (possibly my imagination) and directing her bored gaze down the street.

When exactly had my little girl become a troubled teenager? And, God forbid, when had I become one of those people who yell out, "Oh, don't worry, she's really friendly" just before their dog chomps the calf of some pensioner out for a walk?

"Kathy, I'm so sorry to hear this," I finally said. "We had no idea. Of course, she can't be allowed to come into your yard and go after your chickens. Is Mr. Clucker all right?"

"Yes," she said, "but you've got to do something."

"We will, of course. We need to repair our pen first. But we've been thinking about training, too."

Kathy was finally unleashing Penny.

"You know how she got started," I said, reaching to take Penny by the collar. "Bad situation, the puppy mill. Maybe some trauma there. And now those chimps in the garage have really got her going."

"She was nosing around the chickens before the fire, Nathan."

"Ah. Yeah. I'm really sorry."

"She needs something to do," Kathy said. "She's too smart and active to stay home all day sleeping."

"I guess she needs more than a couple walks a day," I said, kneeling next to Penny, gently pinching the coppery folds of her throat. "Like a hobby. Or a job."

We both looked at Penny, who stood, squirming a bit, and began to shake off the major guilt trip just laid on her by Kathy Chaney. I noticed a tiny feather stuck to the corner of her red lips.

"And exactly what kind of job would that be?" Kathy asked, slowly wrapping the purple leash around her fist.

*****

Only a couple regulars like me populated the barstools at the Cenozoic Brew Pub. The wildfire and smoke and wind had chased away all the tourists. And most of the second-home owners in the swanky Skylandia development were now back in Seattle and Bellevue. These last few years, the movements of people escaping wildfire smoke were as swift and unpredictable as the direction of the smoke itself. Welcome to the era of the fire refugee.

"It's a good start," said Dave, leaning over my shoulder and reading the draft blog post on my laptop. "Maybe shorten it. Or even wait a bit before posting? People are pretty raw right now. Don't need to be preached to, you know?"

I trusted Dave Schmidell. He made great beer and had unusually well-developed listening skills. He also happened to be on top of the fire situation. His wife Muriel worked at the local Forest Service office and had just been promoted to incident commander on the Happy Mountain fire.

"Yeah, could be," I said. "Kind of hate to lose a teaching moment, though."

Dave stood in the doorway leading to the back storeroom. He wiped his hands on a towel and held me in his steady gaze.

"And these fires are not all bad," I continued, turning my attention back to my laptop's screen. "Of course, the loss of life and homes is tragic. No question. I need to say that here in the blog. Tragic. But we better get used to it if we don't change some things."

I took a sip of my second Mosaic IPA, the one Dave had just set down in front of me, and looked again at the draft on my screen. It had expanded since morning. What a time to live! No journal editors to reject my thesis! No costs for publication! Just one man against the world! I already had over 700 followers on my blog.

"Here's the thing, Dave," I said, still gazing at my screen as he moved back behind the bar. "We're going to live with more fire whether we want to or not. For us, short-term, it's a challenge. But for the forest itself and for the animals who evolved in that forest, fire is life. That's their home."

When I looked up, I discovered it wasn't Dave staring at me from behind the bar, but his new bartender. She'd been working here for just a couple weeks. I'd seen her once or twice, but I hadn't talked with her yet. According to Dave, she'd recently moved to La Likt with her son, a senior at La Likt-Patrick High School.

She wore a short-sleeved pink angora sweater above black jeans. "So, fire is good?" she said, tilting her head slightly. A thick braid of blonde hair hung down over her shoulder and dangled above the front pocket of her jeans.

"Fire is beautiful," I said. "It's restorative. Necessary."

"But that beauty is also destructive," she said, leaning into the bar's rounded inner edge, her eyes fixing mine above the laptop. "People die. Houses burn. Surely you don't want that."

"Of course not," I replied in my gentlest voice. "I'm just saying fire has an important role. Almost like rain. Or the sun. We need to learn to live with it."

"Well then, that's better, I guess," she said, a corner of her mouth curling up, amused. "Just making sure you're not a crazy fire guy, ya know." She pressed her lips together and narrowed her eyes as she leaned in closer, a mock examination. "And I know what you mean, actually," she whispered, a crucifix hanging from a gold chain around her neck now banging into the back of my laptop. "Sometimes nature's way includes peripheral damage, right?" She may have winked at me just before I reached for my beer and returned my attention to my laptop.

"Did you know," I heard her say, her voice lowered and suddenly very close to my ear, "that the black-backed woodpecker will only feed on three species of beetles—all of them found only on burnt trees above 15-inches in diameter?"

"Yes!" I practically yelped, beer retreating to coaster and my eyes back on hers. Big blue eyes. Now very close to me. "Have you ever seen one? Dave said you moved up from Arizona."

"Not yet. Would love to though."

"Well," I said, tapping open Merlin, the Cornell University bird app. "You're lucky. There are several stunning burns nearby. Up the Icicle Creek drainage. Out in the hills above Ellensburg. We're very fortunate."

"Dave told me you were a birder," she said.

I spun the laptop partway around so she could see the photos of several male and female three-toeds. She placed an elbow on the bar and leaned in to share a close look.

"Really should go get my glasses," she said, moving in even closer to squint at the screen. I felt some part of her sweater press against my upper arm.

"Just beautiful." She was now flicking the trackpad to scroll and view the photos and distribution maps, clicking on links to mountain pine beetles and engraver beetles.

It was too late to shift my arm away from the pink pressure. That would just call attention to it. We watched several brief woodpecker videos.

Then she opened the black-backed vocalization audios. As she cocked her head away from me to better absorb the low-pitched call note, the very tip of her braid, which was folded back against itself and held in a loose ball with a striped scrunchy, fell into my beer and floated atop the golden foam like a lure on the river.

"My name is Twyla," she sighed, possibly to me, possibly to the birds.

Chapter 3

Beth makes arrangements

John the real estate king caught sight of Penny and me from a half block away. Like everyone else in town, he had something to say. I could tell by the way he stepped off the crumbling curb of the sidewalk, then nimbly course-corrected to intercept us. Impressive for a big man who'd gone through two total knee joint replacements.

"You're making the arrangements?" he thundered as he made his way toward us, one hand slicing the smoky air and the other squeezing the life out of the hand-carved bust of Thomas Jefferson that topped his oak walking stick. It wasn't really a question that needed an answer. Penny and I were standing in front of the town's funeral home.

"Good morning, John," I said wearily. I'd parked my vintage Volkswagen Bug, a birthday gift from Nathan, not more than 50 yards from the funeral home's front door, but already I'd been stopped from entering twice—once by Jamie the hairstylist and then by Sue who owned the bakery. In hushed voices they'd both asked about Paula and Brooklyn. I told them what they already knew— Paula was dead and Brooklyn was missing. Then I added that since Paula had no next of kin with a known address, I was her executor and was making funeral arrangements.

This information evidently was spreading fast.

"It's a crime, a real crime," John fumed. "A senior member of our community and, God help us, a little girl." His voice broke, and he shook his head vigorously. "And we both know it didn't have to happen. If they'd just started fighting the damn fire when it was over the hill in Icicle, it wouldn't have spread down here."

I made my best noncommittal sound, a short "hmm" expelled with plenty of breath behind it. Opinion in town seemed to be running against the Forest Service, which had opted at first to keep the fire under observation. In practice, that meant letting it burn through densely forested land since initial indications pointed to a natural cause: lightning strike. The idea was to let fire restore the forest to its historic number of trees, before Smokey Bear put on his pants and picked up his shovel. But once the wind came up and the fire spread, "under observation" became a very unpopular choice in Sahaptin County. Somebody was likely to lose their job over it. I hoped it wouldn't be my friend Muriel.

"And of course, they didn't have the crews here to fight it," the real estate king continued. "You know all our crews are getting sent to California to fight that Malibu fire. We're on our own up here, as usual. Doesn't matter that we pay taxes too. Especially now that Des Conner's been killed."

"Des Conner? From that British rock band?"

"Yeah. You know, The Loonies? His house went up in the Malibu fire. They found him in it today," John said. "So of course, now all of our Hotshots are getting shipped south to fight fire in California, and good luck to Sahaptin County." He made a disgusted sound in the back of his throat. "Not all men are created equal after all."

It takes a surprisingly long time for some of us to figure that out, I thought.

*****

Paula had made it as easy on me as she could, leaving clear instructions on what to do upon her death: cremation, scatter the ashes, and hold a wake at the Three Bells in Seattle, the place where reporters hung out. The hard part would be tracking down her son and, after that, settling the estate. But I'd worry about that another day. Maybe after we found Brooklyn. My heart lurched at the thought.

What I hadn't told Jamie or Sue or John was that in addition to being Paula's executor, I was also her choice to become Brooklyn's guardian in case disaster befell Paula while James and Chloe were unable to care for their daughter. Before I signed the papers, Nathan and I had discussed the possibility of becoming instant parents at an age when most of our friends' kids were graduating from college or getting married. It brought up a lot of memories that both of us had done everything short of undergoing surgery to avoid. Nevertheless, those old thoughts stormed my consciousness like an angry mob. I can see them now, in their motorcycle boots and makeshift body armor, waving flags and placards and chanting one thing: why don't you have children?

For a dozen years or so, during my reproductive hot zone, it was a question I heard almost every day. Or no, that's not exactly accurate. The question I heard was, "Do you have children?" It's a common enough icebreaker. But once you force the corners of your lips into a tight smile and answer, "No, I don't," the conversation slips and skitters and flails and finally falls through the surface of the now-broken ice. Few people ask the next question, but it hangs around like a bad smell nonetheless: Well then. Why not?

"Why not?" screams the mob in my mind. "What's wrong with you?"

"Is it physical?" yells one particularly unpleasant man wearing Viking's horns. He carries a long knife duct taped to a broomstick.

"Or is it mental?" screams his female partner, who brandishes a naked, plastic babydoll nailed to a garden stake.

Well then. It was mental. And then it was physical.

When Nathan and I married, just out of college and with all the confidence in our own opinions that being young brings, we were sure we didn't want children. Too many kids on the planet already, Nathan said. And if there was a baby in the house, I asked (though I already knew the answer) who would take care of it?

Family, we both said, doesn't have to include two kids and a dog. Better, we said, to move through the world independently.

And then I missed a period.

After a jittery week, I took a home pregnancy test and nearly passed out when the thin blue line that meant "positive" appeared. I sat on the toilet, head between my knees. When I showed the strip to Nathan that evening, his reaction was eerily similar.

"That's a pregnancy test," he pronounced, dropping hard onto one of the second-hand chairs scrabbling for space around the kitchen table in our cramped rental house. "That's a positive pregnancy test." He dropped his head between his knees.

"Congratulations, Mr. Scientist," I said testily. "If you know what's good for you, you won't ask how this happened."

"Well, that's—that's okay," he said. "These things aren't always accurate. I mean, we'll get it confirmed by a doctor, right?"

"Right," I said, very near to tears. "But Nathan, if I am pregnant —"

We stared at each other, and then he said, "We don't have to decide anything tonight, Beth. We've got some time to think about things."

You've heard this story before, so I'll make it quick. I went to the doctor, and I was pregnant. And, as in so many events in life, perception didn't match reality. The day after we had our final answer, it was Nathan who quietly said, "We have options, Beth. Good options. We can go back to how things were, and I'd be happy with that." I remember he removed his baseball cap—he was a San Francisco Giants fan at the time—and then clamped it back down decisively. "Or we can have a baby. And I would be happy with that."

And so we began to entertain the idea of a baby. We walked around our little house, scouting out a corner of the bedroom for a crib. We hunched over our checking account statements—all on paper in those days—and made endless adjustments to our monthly budget. "If it's a girl," I told Nathan one morning before work, "I want to name her after my sister Laura."

Then late one night, my period came on with a vengeance. I know that's a cliché, but that's what all of the blood seemed like: revenge for not wanting a child in the first place. The next morning, I was no longer pregnant. I returned to the doctor and then to a series of doctors, and I learned that should I become pregnant again, the end result would likely be the same.

"Well," said Nathan, tears shining in his eyes. "That's okay. That's okay, Beth, right? That was the original plan, anyway." He furiously scrubbed at his face with his flannel sleeve. "I hate when people say this, but maybe it's for the best." He paused, and repeated, "Maybe it's for the best, Beth?"

"Maybe," I said, because what else was there to say to my taciturn husband, now as close as I'd ever seen him to weeping?

It's taken a while, but a few decades have passed and knowing Nathan and myself as I do, I think that maybe it was for the best. Besides, a woman (or a man or anyone else, for that matter) isn't defined by her fertility. Family doesn't have to be two kids and a dog.

And besides, now we had the dog.

*****

Our funeral home business finished for now, I stuffed Penny into the backseat of the Bug. I took the driver's seat myself, then turned to give my dog a long, cold glare. She gazed back at me through her golden eyes, all innocence.

"You know how to ask to go out, Penny," I said to her. "You learned that a long time ago."

She thrust her floppy ears forward and wrinkled her forehead as if concerned about my sanity.

"You do too know what I'm talking about," I told her. "Doing that on the rug." I clicked my tongue against my teeth. "You embarrassed both of us. And today of all days. As if things weren't hard enough." I turned around and furiously wiped my eyes and nose on the sleeve of my sweatshirt. It's always disconcerting how sadness surfaces in the middle of the most mundane moments—drying the breakfast dishes, walking through the automatic doors at Safeway, lecturing your misbehaving dog. Something reminds you of what you've lost and you struggle all over again to come to terms. I cranked the key harder than was necessary and the Bug started with its usual tooth-rattling clatter.

Penny had been such a sweet puppy. When we brought her home, she seemed almost grateful. At first, she spent a lot of time noisily enjoying her high-calorie dog food and then happily accompanying Nathan to Dave's brew pub, where she'd curl into an adorable ball behind the bar. She'd taken to the leash well and, on her walks, she showed no more than the usual interest in squirrels. She quietly rode in my lap whenever Nathan drove us over the pass and slept peacefully most nights in a nest of blankets next to our bed. I'd had my doubts about adopting a dog born in a busted-down puppy mill, but Penny had proven me wrong.

At least, she had until recently. I'd read that Hungarian Vizslas were sporting dogs and natural hunters. So, I suppose I shouldn't have been surprised that Penny was going after Mr. Clucker or that she'd attacked what was left of my oldest pair of leather hiking boots. But I was dismayed by her sudden lack of basic manners. Maybe Kathy was right. Maybe she did need a job.

We chugged our way the two miles west to the town of Patrick, home of the local animal shelter as well as the region's only bookstore-slash-coffee house, craft distillery, and farmer's market. In short, Patrick had all the makings of a town on the move. I'll admit many of us in La Likt were jealous of Patrick, with its shabby chic charm and its robust second-home market.

Of course, right now Patrick was also two miles closer to the Happy Mountain fire. The fire was slowly coming under containment, but the sky above Patrick was a murky reddish brown and a fine, gray powder—ash from the burning forest—coated everything that stood still long enough. In the town's most popular bar, which claimed to be the oldest continuously operating tavern in the state, the usual bikers sat on the usual stools drinking the usual beers, but otherwise Patrick was devoid of its summertime tourists. Penny and I cruised the main street, which is fronted by quaint, weathered-wood buildings housing restaurants and boutiques. You have to go down the road to La Likt to find the Dollar Store and the Dairy Queen. We took a few minutes to watch the steady parade of vehicles hauling lawn chairs, bicycles, kayaks, and barbecues, all headed away from the lake campground toward the interstate.

"Go west, young Sprinter van," I said. Penny shook her head vigorously, setting her ears and tags flying.

When we pulled up in front of the animal shelter, I clipped on Penny's leash and secured her to the bicycle rack out front, where I could keep an eye on her from the front windows. No way was I taking her inside, where she might incite a riot among the shelter's guests. Our arrival already seemed to have been noticed by one internee, who let out an anguished howl.

"Winston!" a plump, graying woman in a pair of heavy-duty work pants demanded as I pushed open the door. "That's enough now!" The dog quieted. Anybody would have.

I gave the woman my toothiest smile. "You," I said, "are someone I need to know."

"Well, then," she said. "Speak!"

I was impressed and a little intimidated by the authority in her tone. "It's my dog," I obediently answered, gesturing outside. Penny was stretching her leash as far as it would go, having taken a not altogether friendly interest in a baby lashed to a stroller that was bumping along the gravel road out front.

"Lately, she's regressed in her training," I explained. "She always walked well on leash." I suddenly felt it was imperative that the woman understand Penny was a good dog at heart. "She knew 'sit' and 'stay' and 'go potty.'" I paused and we both watched as Penny's lips curled into a snarl.

"She never used to do that!" I blurted. "She never used to try to kill things, for Chr—Pete's sake!"

Having worked in a newsroom most of my life, I'd picked up some bad habits when it came to dropping F-bombs and taking in vain the name of the person most people in Sahaptin County considered their lord and savior. I figured it wasn't friendly, this casual way I had of offending people, so lately I was trying out a variety of milder linguistic options.

The gray-haired woman nodded. "Squirrels?" she asked.

"Chickens," I replied.

"Has anything in her routine changed recently?"

I thought about it. "What with the fire scares this summer, we haven't been walking her as much," I admitted. "But we leave her in her dog run when we can't take her with us so she can get some exercise."

"She's spending more time on her own?"

"Probably," I said. "Yes."

The woman nodded decisively. "She's a Vizsla, right? So, she's a Velcro dog."

"Velcro dog?" I repeated.

"She needs to stick with her people." The woman turned, grabbed a piece of paper off the counter behind her, and offered it to me. "Don't leave her alone so much. Find something you can do together," she said. "Something useful, if possible, like this training class for search and rescue dogs."

I looked at the paper. "Your Dog can be a Hero," it read. "Sahaptin County Search and Rescue." An informational meeting was scheduled for the following Saturday.

"Isn't she too old for this kind of training?" I asked.

The woman considered Penny, who now seemed to be gnawing her right front paw. "Maybe," she said. "But maybe not. She's a real beauty, and Vizslas are smart. Why not give her a chance?"

*****

My phone rang just as I got Penny situated in the back of the Volkswagen. The name that flashed on my screen instantly made me feel like I needed a tall Gin & Tonic.

I swiped at the green button. "Nigel," I said.

"Mary Beth!" said my editor. "I am so glad we've connected at last. One never knows how well the signal will travel so far from—" He considered his words. "That is, in an area that's been so recently settled."

I briefly considered informing him that the area had been settled by the ancestors of the Sahaptin people at least as long ago as his beloved London, but after working with Nigel for almost a year as The Informant's western U.S. correspondent, I've learned it's usually best to get him off the phone fast. Gives him less chance to come up with one of his "absolutely original" story ideas.

"What's up?" I asked.

"We've been following the news of your fires," he said.

This surprised me. It didn't seem the usual thing for a London tabloid. "You've been following the news of our fires?" I asked. "Including the one in Dave's dumpster?"

"What?" he said. "No, the fires in California. Specifically, the one in Malibu. Des Conner's a goner, you know."

Of course. The British rock star.

"It's a big story here, Mary Beth. A big story. But, of course, we're always looking for a fresh angle. That's why I'm in Seattle."

I gasped involuntarily. Nigel was in Seattle? This was not good news.

"We have a team in L.A. now," Nigel said, and I wondered how hard he'd worked to get on that team. If I knew Nigel, Seattle was a fallback position, and it was a long fall.

"Malibu, that's the obvious thing," he said dismissively. "You and I understand that. But you and I, we never go for the obvious story. So! I'm coming to La Likt. I'll be there tonight."

On top of everything else, I didn't need Nigel trailing me around, demanding proper mugs of tea, clean towels, and sensational copy. I tried to keep the panic out of my voice. "Nigel, you've been to La Likt," I said, glancing around me. "It's not even as happening as Patrick. You're sure this is where the story is?"

"Not everything is in Malibu," he said. "Well, perhaps most things are, but think of it! We can call the package 'Wildfires of the West!' Or 'Blaze in the Boondocks!' Or perhaps just, 'Inferno!'"

"'Blaze in the Boondocks?'" I repeated.

"We're in the concept stage, Mary Beth. I'll see you at your charming cabin in a couple of hours."

"I'll make you a reservation at the Sno-Cap," I sputtered as my phone went black. I gazed down at it, disbelieving, and it nearly vibrated out of my hand—one long shuddering jump followed by two shorts, the signal of Sahaptin County Emergency Services.

"Fires reported on upper La Likt River," my screen read. "Lake Cabins neighborhood under mandatory evacuation. Leave immediately."

Chapter 4

Nathan picks up a nickname

Watching a friend at their workplace is always interesting. Before your eyes, they morph into a half-stranger with new skills and vocabulary. Perhaps even a surprising aptitude for bureaucratic nitpicking. It can give you a new appreciation. Keep you curious.

Muriel Schmidell was at work, and it was a big deal. After the incident commander for the Happy Mountain fire was sent to Southern California to lead those efforts, Muriel was promoted. Tonight, she had her game face on and her ranger trousers pressed.

I'm pretty sure she saw me at the rear of the hall when she came in, but she sailed right past me. Muriel and I know each other well, not least because her husband Dave owns and operates Cenozoic Brewing. Also, Beth and I hike with Dave and Muriel all the time. Nonetheless she ignored me. No hint she knew me. She was at work.

I was at the table with the free cookies, chatting up Twyla and trying to stuff a couple of napkin-wrapped peanut butter sandies into my jacket pocket for later that night. The guy Beth and I refer to as The Italian was back there too, doggedly trying to refill his Styrofoam cup from the stainless steel coffee carafe, though it only burbled and burbled.

"Looks like we killed that one," said Twyla cheerfully, hoping The Italian would take the hint and desist. When he didn't, she turned back to me, tilted her head, jacked up her eyebrows, and gave me a loopy smile, which I interpreted as a comment on the eccentricities of certain Europeans.

Over Twyla's shoulder I spotted Beth standing near the stage up front, talking with Cassie.

"Hey, Glenn. Come on over here," Twyla called to a buff young guy standing nearby. He looked a bit lost. He had long black hair pulled back in a ponytail and Clark Kent-type black-framed glasses. Maybe in his late teens or early twenties? Christ, he could be thirty. Hard to tell. Kids mature faster today.

"This is Nathan Drake," Twyla said. "He runs the High Country Crapper project I told you about. Nathan, this is my son Glenn."

"Your work is so important," the boy said as we shook hands. "I bet you take a lot of shit, so to speak, for what you're doing, but it's one of those neglected corners of the public health space."

What was this kid, a Stanford MBA? "Well, thanks, Glenn," I said, "I'm flattered that you took the time to learn about it."

"I'd like to study limnology down at U.C. Davis after high school. The intersection of water quality and recreation. That's my thing."

Impressive. Rare. Why hesitate? "Well, hey, my associate Charlie is leaving soon. If you're interested in some work experience before you head down to California—we could call it a paid internship—give me a call."

He glanced at his mom, then awkwardly stuck out his hand again. "That would be great, Mr. Drake. I would love that."

"You'd be helping me out," I said before we all scattered to our seats.

This was the second fire-related community meeting of the week. Same venue as the first: the La Likt Senior Center. The only other hall in town large enough for this crowd was the Eagles Club but that old brick building was sway-walled and irredeemably infused with the scent of rodentia in-situ.

So, there we sat on folding chairs arrayed across the linoleum floor of the senior center lunchroom, waiting as the fire officials were clipped with microphones, the situation evidently dire enough for them to ditch the hand-held mics. The crowd was twice as large and three times as noisy as that of the previous meeting. Beth, her editor Nigel Turner, and I were seated near the back in case we decided to duck out. Most of the updates and maps were already available online. We definitely wanted the latest news, but these community things had a way of being hijacked by the loudest voice in the room.

"Those lunch offerings sound pretty good," I said to Beth, looking over at the old-style signboard above the cafeteria counter. "I think Monday's turkey and biscuits casserole might hit the spot, no?"

"I'd stick with the Thursday bingo burger if I were you," she said. "Less chance for error." Good to see her joking reflex in order.

"Now, tell me if I'm wrong, Nathan," chimed Nigel, that turd, as he absentmindedly scanned the crowd, "you would qualify for these government subsidized senior meals, would you not?"

"I believe any and all are welcome here, Nigel," I said.

"Ah yes. But I'm sure these nutritious selections—I note the five-cheese carrot and pea casserole in particular—would be especially beneficial for a man of your years." He said this while continuing his predator's survey of the room and the methodical feeding of his beak from a stack of M&M-embedded cookies on his lap.

Thank God we had no room for this man in our cabin during his open-ended tenure here in La Likt. No idea how Beth can stand to work with him.

All the fire honchos on stage, though hailing from different galaxies of the wildfire-fighting cosmos, shared the look: startlingly clean and white skin, muscular but slightly puffy bods barely constrained within their uniforms—observe the neck folds over the collar—shaved round heads, and black wrap-around sunglasses parked atop those signature gleaming domes. In nature, wildly different species sometimes adopt the same body structures or behaviors if they share the same environment. Think sharks and dolphins. As I mused on this apparent case of firefighter convergent evolution, a voice resounded from the center aisle.

"Let's get this show on the road, boys," roared Roger Thorp. He was standing tall in his Stetson, surrounded by a few acolytes, most likely fans of his old-school conservative radio show, which he broadcast every Tuesday and Thursday out of his home in the hills above Ellensburg. "Some of us aren't getting paid by the hour here. We've got homes to protect."

I noticed that Twyla, seated up near the front, clapped tepidly at Thorp's remarks. So did about half the others in the room. Twyla wore a white silk shawl around her shoulders and her braid was loosely coiled atop her head. I felt good about helping her little family—a job for Glenn, some fun birding for her—like I was finally making some community connections. They were new to town and obviously just scraping by. Dave told me Twyla had taken on another part-time job, as a reporter for the local paper. He said they lived in what locals call the "divorce court" apartments on the road between La Likt and Patrick.

"Almost set, Roger," said Muriel, who was tonight's moderator. One of the reasons she was plucked for this assignment, Dave hinted, was her ability to identify and neutralize a loudmouth like Thorp. Community relations, aka making nice with nut jobs, was one of those surprising on-the-job skills that we were witnessing tonight in our pal Muriel.

"In fact," said Muriel, in full welcome mode, sweeping the room with her eyes, "everybody, please have a seat. More up front here."

With that, Muriel introduced the sheriff and the three Homo firefightus specimens who'd give us updates on evacuations, casualties, and property damage. Muriel herself would provide info on containment, wind forecasts, and timelines for residents to return to their homes—or, sadly, perhaps to their blackened chimneys and melted appliances. A startlingly young woman from the Red Cross would detail the temporary housing situation at the high school. One other guy, even whiter than the firefighters but skinnier, sat at the end of the stage in a light-colored suit and pale blue shirt sans necktie. He looked slightly miffed at not being introduced.

The Happy Mountain fire, we learned first, was 67 percent contained.

"Residents on the hill and in the La Likt Ridge townhomes will be allowed back in when it's safe," said Sheriff Clint Peters, his gun, radio, cuffs, and badge all jangling as he paced the stage. "The crews are getting close, but those hot spots need work. Your patience is appreciated. The cause is still undetermined."

Thorp pounced immediately. "I hope you're looking for the real cause."

"It's under investigation, Roger," said Muriel reassuringly.

"Well, be sure to ask your own crews about it. They were up there the day before for prescribed burns. Maybe a little spilled diesel from the drip torch?"

Everybody looked at Muriel. "That's not accurate," she said evenly. "The Forest Service has not engaged in prescribed burns up there."

"Not what I heard," muttered a lanky guy in a Mariners baseball cap who sat up front. He glanced back at Thorp, a few seats behind him, and then scrunched down into his seat, pulling his cap lower. The crowd murmured.

"Or maybe one of your crew was looking to be a hero?" Thorp barked helpfully at Muriel. "Set the thing. Put it out. Look essential. Happens all the time."

Muriel let that one mulch in its own obvious stink as she glanced at her notes. The crowd, tight-lipped faces kept forward, was not touching that one either.

Undeterred, Thorp popped upright, knocking his metal chair back, and spoke as if at last he could unburden himself of the plain truth he had come to deliver. "Those of us who live around here in the hills know—fact certain—that Eastern Washington Power is doing a piss poor job of clearing trees from around their lines."

He pointed to the man in the beige suit at the end of the stage. "More than likely one of those trees that should've been cut fell over in the wind and started this whole mess. Right? You find your downed line yet? What've you got to say, Spokane?"

The guy stood up with an urgency that matched Thorp's, swept a hand through his sandy hair, and cleared his throat, ready to defend himself and his power company. Muriel held up her hand to stop him.

"Listen everybody, these are great questions," she said. "The cause of the Happy Mountain fire is under investigation, and we hope to have some answers soon. As it is, we've got a lot to get through tonight. You all want to know about the La Likt River fires, right? We'll have the breakout sessions at the end of the night where you can ask anyone about anything you want. Mr. Brantley from Eastern Washington Power in Spokane will be here, too."

Ah, the breakout sessions. Where dissent goes to die. Good move, Muriel.

"You're using Mexican subcontractors to clear the lines," yelped a guy in a cowboy hat seated near Thorp. "They aren't up to the job."

"What'd you expect from a crew out of Yakima," Thorp snorted. "They don't know a holy thing about these woods." He rattled his folding chair back in place and collapsed into it with a heavy sigh. "God almighty," he chuckled to those around him, "just look at those little Nissan trucks they're driving."

I'd listened to Thorp's broadcasts—"The Voice of Colockum Ridge"—while I worked on our new garage. I considered these forays into Thorp radio as opposition research. Giving the other side a chance to make their case. Seems to me I do a lot of that type of listening these days. Mostly a liberal thing.

Anyway, my unrepentant take on Thorp? He was basically a latter-day Rush Limbaugh resurrected and transplanted to rural Central Washington. Full of anti-government tirades about land and water rights. Spouting off about those traitorous environmentalists. Dedicated to unfettered access to assault rifles, of course, but not health care. The wisdom of the rancher. Seattle: city of the damned.

Sheriff Peters, whom we had nearly forgotten during Thorp's interruption, took advantage of the momentary silence as Muriel thumbed her notes. "One more thing, folks," he said. "We do appreciate your staying clear of the evac zones. It's hard, I know. But it's just not safe."

Cassie leapt from her chair in the front row. "Sheriff, when can I get back up to my place to search for the girl who refused to come down the hill?"

The sheriff was slow to respond. "You mean the little girl, Brooklyn?"

"No, no," Cassie said. "I meant our oldest female chimp. Holly Chimpanzee. She just refused to get in her cage. She's stubborn. I had to leave her at the sanctuary. When can I go back up?"

"Oh yeah, I heard about that," he responded. "I'm sorry, but we got folks with missing pets and animals all over. Can't allow anyone back in yet."

Cassie turned a beseeching face to Muriel and slowly sat.

Sheriff Peters also glanced over at Muriel, blinked twice, then tilted his chin up and hooked his thumbs inside his belt. From below his luxuriant mustache, two beaver teeth emerged briefly to press on his lower lip. "Now, ya'll know we got this other situation with little Brooklyn Novak still missing. Paula's granddaughter. The fire burned hot at her cabin and, well, it's just a tough, tough search. The structures and cars. The forensics folks—" he faltered. "We're still looking."

No doubt realizing the grizzly impressions that the sheriff's utterances might be leaving, Muriel jumped in. "We're looking all over, in fact, aren't we, Sheriff? A wide area. Let's keep hoping and praying. Sahaptin County Search and Rescue is on it."

The sheriff nodded.

"Thank you, Sheriff Peters," said Muriel, eager to move on. "By the way, if anybody wants to volunteer on that search, keep an eye on our Forest Service social media accounts."

"Oh, but one final thing," said the sheriff. "Brooklyn's parents. Kind of out of the picture for years. We want to locate them. Just due diligence. All part of ensuring that Brooklyn is safe. Wherever she is. If anybody has information on the whereabouts of James Novak or —"

"I'm right here, man."

The raspy voice coming from the back of the room belonged to a man in red sneakers, green wide-wale cords, and a huge dark blue down jacket. His hair was shaved short on the sides, a few gouges to the underlying skin apparent. It was completely unmown on top, a real rat's nest thing going on up there. I spotted a short stack of M&M cookies in his hand making a stealthy retreat up his puffy sleeve.

"And I didn't kidnap Brooklyn, if that's what you're thinking," he added.

Beth stood up and moved toward the back of the room. "Of course not, James," she said. "I'm so glad you're here. Let's go out front with the sheriff to get you up to date."

The sheriff took the hint and nodded to Muriel before he moseyed down the aisle and out of the door along with Beth and James.

Nigel, who'd been taking notes in his skinny notebook, turned back to the stage and said to no one in particular, "Your town meetings are so entertaining. Tension. Personalities. Unexpected twists." Waiting for the next bit of small-town drama, he absentmindedly deployed his notebook to brush a lapful of cookie crumbs to the floor.

Another Forest Service official stepped forward to report on the new fires. The flames lined both sides of the state highway that hugs the La Likt River all the way up to the lake, he told us. An eight-mile line of fires of various sizes over varying terrain. Several of the roadside blazes had blown up in the afternoon winds and run uphill to Yellow Knife Ridge. Every little riverside and lake cabin as well as all the newer, 5,000-square foot stone-and-glass palaces located high on the hillside were under strict evacuation orders. A total of 355 homes at risk. No containment. No known cause.

"Pretty obvious," yelled the guy in the Mariners hat. "That westside couple in their Mercedes camping van were dragging a tow chain all along that road." Many in the crowd exchanged looks and nods, most of them well aware that sparks from tow chains dragging off back bumpers were a textbook source of ignition for wildfires in the west.

The firefighters on stage looked noncommittal and Thorp broke the silence. "Cop pulled them over headed west on I-90 just 20 minutes after all those river fires got started."

"Let's talk after the meeting, Roger," said Muriel, showing a bit of wear.

"We got our own fire investigator, Honey," Thorp added, tossing his head toward a well-dressed man with a jet black goatee who sat a row up. "Amazing how fast the private sector moves." Thorp's investigator straightened his back, gave his employer a polite nod, and perched in his chair as erect and still as a night heron on the hunt.

After all eyes were on him, the man stood, tugged down on his elegant suit jacket, and spoke formally, as if addressing a jury. "Dr.

LaVonne Heath," he said. "Stanford University. My specialty is using advanced scientific techniques and statistical Bayesian modeling to identify the proximate causes of wildfires. In the instance of the La Likt River Complex, I would estimate the confidence interval for the hypothesis that the tow chain initiated the fire to be well within the commonly accepted standard deviation of 95 percent certainty."

He cocked his goateed chin just a few degrees, first to the right and then to the left, as if watching for minnows in the muck. Sensing no rebuttals, the little professor returned to his perch.

"There you go," said Thorp.

"I don't know why they all haven't been arrested," said the Mariners fan, looking first at Thorp, then at Muriel, and then—what the hell is this?—turning completely around and directing his deep-set eyes right at me. Once he had my attention, he gave me a nod, a half-smile, and turned back to face the speaker.

"Why, that fellow could be your double, Nathan," said Nigel, leaning in and jabbing me with his elbow. "The emaciated build. The advanced years. The facial scruff. Even the tattered baseball cap."

I reached involuntarily for my cap. I hated to admit it, but the Brit twit had a point. The man was indeed my doppelgänger. Beth and I had spotted him around town recently, even jokingly referred to him as the D-word because of his eerie resemblance to yours truly. But what Beth didn't know—and what I only sketchily began to recall as those mournful, familiar eyes bored into me at close range—was that I had actually met him years ago.

Hadn't I?

*****

The presentation finally wrapped and the fire officials decamped to card tables for the breakout sessions. I approached the table where

Muriel stood answering questions and tried to catch her eye. But she was swamped. Or didn't see me. Or, again, avoided me.

When Nigel and I emerged from the senior center, Beth and James were deep in their confab with Sheriff Peters. Nigel marched off across the parking lot to collar the freelance fire investigator as the man lowered himself into a white Tesla, while I approached Beth and James.

"So, you'll let us know if you hear from her," Sheriff Peters was saying.

"Like I said, she might have got a ride up last week. But maybe not. I've been keeping up with treatment at Swedish NorthPoint, but she kind of let that go and I haven't seen much of her. Could still be in Seattle. Could be anywhere."

"But, if Chloe did come up here," the lawman said, "she'd want to see her child, right?"

"No other reason," the younger man replied. "Sure. Maybe."

"And she knew Brooklyn was up at the Happy Mountain cabin?"

"Yeah. With her grandmother, like always. But listen, my mom knew Chloe wanted to see Brooklyn whenever she could. There was the restraining order, but they had an informal arrangement. Meeting at Cassie's place."

"You mean the chimp sanctuary?" Sheriff Peters asked.

"Yeah, just a couple times," James responded.

To his credit, the sheriff gave James plenty of time to consider any further comment.

"But everything was relaxed there, it was cool," he finally added. "Neutral ground. Always supervised by Cassie."

"But to your knowledge," the sheriff carefully enunciated as if for the official record, although he sure wasn't taking notes, "Chloe was not up there the night of the fire?"

"That's correct," James responded.

The young man was taking a risk by revealing these visits to the sheriff. It was an indication, I thought, of his level of concern about his daughter. I didn't know how James Novak could be comfortable in that XXXL down jacket on such a warm evening. At close range, you could see the damage of street life in his face and hands. He looked almost as old as me. But mostly he seemed tired and sad.

Beth had known James since he was six years old. In the way one follows the progress of a friend's beloved child, she knew about his little league career, his triumphs at Queen Anne Elementary School and Ballard High, and his sudden and brief enthusiasms for anime, guitar, and silent films. She knew less about what put him on the streets. It must be eating her up to see him like this.

"James," said Beth, pausing to give his defenses a moment to ease up, "is there anyone Chloe knows up here? Anybody she might stay with?"

"She prefers camping these days," he responded.

"Well," I said, looking the young man in his icteric eyes, "I hope you'll stay with us while you're here. We've got some other visitors in the spare bedroom and out in the garage right now, but the couch is available."

*****

When Beth, James, Cassie, and I returned to the cabin and piled out of the Subaru, those other visitors in the garage were in complete uproar. Hoots and shrieks resounded from within the corrugated metal walls. In the front yard, Penny stood inside the small pen-within-a-broken-pen I had cobbled together for her, trembling with fear and excitement.

The cabin's front door was splintered and standing open. Inside, the dining room hutch was flat on its face. Beth's family china spilled across the floor. Drawers and closets had been ransacked.

Outside, Penny joined the chimps in a good old-fashioned howl fest while Beth stood motionless near the broken dishes, right hand covering her mouth.

James managed to half-close our damaged front door. "Check it out," he said.

On the hallway wall behind the door, in fluorescent orange, was a spray-painted message:

"Burn in Hell, Peckerwood."

Part 2: The La Likt River Complex

Chapter 5

Beth lets go of the leash

"Chimps and humans," said Nigel, goosing the gas pedal in the rental SUV, "we're nearly identical genetically, you know." We lurched leftward into the interstate's passing lane and, as we blew past a Toyota, Nigel bestowed a languid salute upon the astonished driver.

"Okay," I said. "I don't know what that has to do with training Penny in search and rescue, but I'm fairly sure you'll tell me."

My editor had been in town for less than 48 hours and already we'd fallen into the pattern we'd set when we met. We'd both been chasing a story—and a missing heiress—along the Pacific Crest Trail, and once I'd beaten Nigel to the girl, he was quickly convinced that we made the perfect team. Sure, it was awfully convenient timing for him, but afterward he put me on retainer and I was happy to get the work, even though I thought our potential as a team was severely limited. He saw things one way and I saw them the other and together we were in a state of constant irritation.

"I mean to point out that animals are more intelligent than you give them credit for," Nigel said, "including your dog. I can only hope that the instructor at this search training sees her potential as clearly as I do." In the row of seats behind us, Penny opened her jaws wide and snapped them shut again in a half-yawn, half-sneeze.

"And from what Cassie said at dinner last night, Holly Chimpanzee has more common sense than—" He took his left hand from the Dreadnought's steering wheel and waved his bony fingers slowly, conjuring the metaphor. "More common sense, let's say, than a person with a positively irrational love for woodpeckers. About which I also learned a massive amount at dinner last night."

I had to admit, it had been an enlightening evening. In fact, the last couple of days had been a little too interesting for my tastes. Once we returned from the fire meeting and found our cabin vandalized, it took Cassie a full hour to calm the chimps. It had taken longer than that for Nathan to calm me.

"We should call the sheriff and get this documented," I said as Nathan and I gazed at the threat splashed across our cabin wall in bright orange paint. Burn in Hell, Peckerwood. It made me shiver to think Nathan's musing about woodpeckers had made someone angry enough to defile our home. Or maybe what had angered our assailant wasn't so much Nathan's concern for birds as it was his seeming disregard for the people who lived in their habitat. I could imagine how we looked to whoever did this: trespassers from the human wasteland west of the mountains, here to force our beliefs upon them. Woodpeckers, that is, over their way of life. I could understand how that might make a person feel. "Positively diminished," as Nigel said last night, right before heading to his motel room.

But, given the current political climate, I still thought we should call the sheriff.

"Let's not make a big deal out of a few broken dishes and some paint," Nathan had said. "I'll take some pictures of the damage. That's documentation enough." He turned and started toward our unfinished garage, where Cassie was serenading the chimps with an off-key rendition of "Twinkle, Twinkle Little Star." Penny trotted happily behind Nathan, excited about the job ahead. "I think we've got some plywood around somewhere," Nathan said to her. "Enough to get that door boarded up for now."

I sighed. In general, my husband is finished with discussion much sooner than I am. Unless the topic is one of his favorites—water quality, beer, woodpeckers—he's pretty much talked out after a sentence or two. His father is the same way. Their family motto should read, "nothing more need be said."

"Hold on, Nathan," I yelled, nipping along behind Penny's happily waggling rear end. Neither she nor my husband slowed their pace. "Whoever it was that got into the house, how do we know they didn't take something?" I stopped to catch my breath. "Your Gore-Tex jacket isn't on its usual hook by the door," I lobbed at his retreating back. "Your Queen Anne High School baseball hat isn't there, either."

That stopped him.

"You can't get those hats anymore," he said.

"I know," I said.

"That's just low, taking my hat," he said, starting back toward the cabin.

*****

"We all know chimpanzees are intelligent," Nigel was droning as I brought my attention back to the Dreadnought, the interstate, and our appointment at search and rescue training. "But are they actually better able to read the mood of the community than some humans?" He drummed his fingers against the steering wheel triumphantly. "The answer is yes, Mary Beth! It seems that your husband's attempt at journalism and the resulting damage to your rustic home would prove it."

"Oh, Je . . . jeepers, Nigel," I said. "Give it a rest." He tossed me a confused look. "Jeepers?" he silently mouthed.

I leaned forward and flicked on the radio, scrolling through the Christian stations at the lower frequencies in a hopeless effort to pick up the Spokane NPR affiliate.

"And all we want to know is," a familiar baritone set the Dreadnought's speakers to humming, "who's setting our land on fire? We'll take care of the rest."

"Hey," I said, "it's that guy from the fire meetings—Roger Thorp."

"Patriots," Thorp pronounced, "we're going to have to stop this ourselves. We're going to have to take this so-called investigation into our own hands, right here from our command center on Colockum Ridge. Because the jumbucks in Olympia aren't going to help us. They're too busy sending our firefighters to California."

"Jumbucks?" Nigel asked. I waved a hand to shush him.

"So, let's review our suspects," Thorp continued. "We got the U.S. Forest Circus taking our money and working against us, as usual. We got the power company hiring illegals, supposedly to inspect their lines, but I think we all know what they're really doing out there. More on that later."

Thorp took a deep breath and I could just about see him shaking his head in a fit of disgust. "We got numbskulls—and that's the nicest thing I can call them—spreading fire all the way down the La Likt River."

He raised his voice for emphasis. "And finally," he bayed, "we got some crazy peckerwood who thinks burned trees are good for the birdies." He let out a contemptuous laugh. "I know he sounds like some kind of harmless hippie, folks, but believe me, that's just who you've got to look out for."

"Peckerwood?" Sweat began to moisten my forehead just at the hairline. "He's talking about Nathan!"

"So, what do you say, Sahaptin County? Who's going to step up and help us put a stop to these fires? Check in tomorrow for more Straight Talk from Colockum Ridge, and don't forget—keep 'em locked and loaded."

We drove on a few miles in silence while I fretted over my husband's reputation and safety. Finally, Nigel said, "I believe this is our exit." Two fingers resting on the bottom of the steering wheel, he wedged the SUV into the right lane and piloted us off the interstate, immune to the sound of a semi's air brakes shuddering behind us. We took the offramp at speed and I heard Penny's nails skitter across the leather seat behind me.

"Holly Chimpanzee and Brooklyn Novak went missing around the same time," Nigel explained as we entered the roundabout leading to Sahaptin High School. He ignored a pickup in the inner lane, its driver waving her arm out of the window in an effort to exit the traffic circle before she'd have to go around again. "Holly Chimpanzee had experience with babies. Cassie said she'd had four of them during her time as a research subject." He smoothly exited the traffic circle, shooting the pickup driver a triumphant thumbs up and pulling into the high school's parking lot. "Brooklyn visited the chimp sanctuary many times," he continued, "and Holly was her favorite."

We took a parking spot beside a truck loaded with four tidy dog kennels. I looked back at Penny, feeling guilty that she had no crate to ride in. "Meeting's about to start, Nigel," I said.

"Aren't you in the least curious about what happened to Brooklyn?"

I felt my face flush and my hands ball into fists. "Brooklyn Novak was," I corrected myself, "Brooklyn Novak is the granddaughter of one of my best friends. And in case you haven't noticed, I've been planning that friend's funeral, Nigel."

"I know that," he began, but I interrupted him. "Paula," my voice broke and I had to start again. "Paula took in Brooklyn when her granddaughter needed her, and she died trying to get that little girl to safety."

I leaned over the gear box as Nigel flattened himself against the armrest on the opposite door. I noted with satisfaction that the position looked painful. "So yes, Nigel. I care about what happened to Brooklyn. I believe we'll find her, maybe with someone who left the area during the fire. Maybe in Seattle with her mom. What I don't believe is that a chimpanzee somehow spirited her off through a firestorm and has kept her alive for almost a week. So don't bother telling me your latest, half-ass fire fantasy." I paused to take a breath. "Dammit!," I sputtered. "I mean half-baked!"

"Ehm," Nigel said nervously. "Yes, I'm hearing you." I fell back onto my side of the Dreadnought and tried to concentrate on the breathing exercises my yoga teacher taught me after I fell out of a crow pose and shouted the F-word in class.

"Still," he said, "is it possible that Holly saved Brooklyn?" He rubbed his long fingers together. "That would be a story! Better than a dead rocker who hadn't charted since 2001."

"Nigel." I gave him a warning look.

"Yes, I know, may he rest in the balm of the lord or what have you," Nigel said. "But after meeting Cassie, I read a bit about chimps. Jane Goodall's website."

"Oh, here we go."

"Chimps can care for human children, Mary Beth! That is, after a fashion. If they have strong enough motivation."

I huffed out of the Dreadnought and slammed the door for emphasis. The effect was blunted somewhat when I immediately had to reopen it to retrieve my bag and Penny's leash, and then set to dragging the reluctant dog out of the backseat.

Inside the high school gym, about a dozen people accompanied by an assortment of dogs had gathered on the far end of the bleachers.

"They mostly look like Labs to me," I whispered to Nigel. He gave me a blank look. "The dogs," I added. "Not the people."

Penny's nails clicked across the hardwood floor—I hadn't clipped them, and I wondered if that would be a mark against us—and we sat down as soon as possible on the cold aluminum benches at floor level. I was relieved when Penny did her butt-hovering, semi-sit thing for only a few seconds before touching down completely. She looked around tentatively, brow furrowed, then seemed to decide to ignore the other dogs.

In front of our group stood a petite woman wearing a fluorescent orange safety vest. She was accompanied by a sleek black Lab in a similar outfit. "Welcome, everyone, to our informational meeting for K9 SAR teams," she said. Her dog sat directly at her right foot, its eyes never leaving her face.

Before the woman could continue, Nigel raised his hand and churned the air lazily until she reluctantly recognized him.

"Ehm," he said. "I'd like to know if there's ever been a case of a dog finding a baby, or say, a two-year-old."

"Absolutely," the woman replied. "That's the image most people have of K9 SAR teams from TV and movies—going out into the woods and finding a child. But our teams do much, much more. As I'm about to tell—"

"So, if the dog," Nigel interrupted, "sorry, that is, if the K9 can find a child, could an equally intelligent animal, for example, a chimpanzee, do the same?"

The petite woman looked confused. "We're discussing K9 SAR teams here today, sir," she said.

"Yes, but if a dog—a K9—can search for and rescue a child, doesn't it make sense that a clearly more intelligent animal, like our cousin the chimpanzee, would be even more successful at caring for a baby in the wilderness?" He jabbed me in the ribs with his pointy elbow. "Say, even for a week?"

By now, the K9 handlers in attendance had all turned to stare at us. The crack about chimps being more intelligent than dogs hadn't gone down well. The petite woman scowled, clearly at the end of her patience.

"Look," she said, "I don't know about chimpanzees, but our K9s and their handlers are highly trained for search and rescue. We train together with our K9s for literally thousands of hours to develop search skills, and we train after that to keep those skills current. Only a small percentage of dogs and handlers—the most serious and dedicated—become K9 SAR teams."

"Yes, very admirable," Nigel said. "But have you considered using other animals?" Unable to meet the eyes of the other K9 owners, I looked down and noticed Penny beginning to fidget. Suddenly she got to her feet and assumed a familiar, squatting position.

"Oh crap!" I gasped. "Not again!"

*****

On the way back to La Likt, Nigel took an unexpected turn off the roundabout. "Just taking a drive out to Colockum Ridge," he said. "See what we can see."

The Dreadnought cruised I-90 east, exited at the little city of Kittitas, and then bumped north on a disintegrating two-lane county road bordered by sage and drying grasses. The country down valley from La Likt is open, with only occasional clumps of evergreens, so it was easy to pick up the white glow of floodlights about half-way up the ridge ahead of us. We sped along until we ran out of pavement and Nigel flipped on the high beams, illuminating alternating dark and light ridges of dusty washboard road stretching into the distance.

"Evidently the road hasn't been graded this year," I observed. "Or in the last ten years."

Nigel eased the SUV onto the dirt, then gunned the engine so forcefully that Penny skittered backward into the second row of passenger seats and I gripped the door handle as if my survival instinct had finally kicked in.

"It's a car hire." Nigel's voice, along with the rest of him, bounced up and down in time with the ridges in the road. "May as well get where we're going."

As we approached the lights, I counted a half-dozen vehicles in the drive—some that looked operable, some that were sunk to their rusting hubs in the fine, white dust. The cars were parked at right angles to a sprawling, single-level home with mud-splashed beige stucco siding. Aluminum foil covered the inside of the picture windows framing the faded front door, and antennas poked toward the sky at crazy angles from the patchy roof. A satellite dish pointing east sat like a sentinel among the sage in the side yard. As we pulled through a break in the chain-link fence surrounding the property, three men and a woman emerged from between the vehicles. Two of the men were chunky in the going-to-fat way of former high school football stars and one of them was wiry, like Nathan. The woman held up her left hand, motioning us to stop. Her right hand was occupied with a gun.

"You lost," she said as if stating a fact, and for a fraction of a second, I thought she meant we'd failed at a competition that I hadn't realized we'd joined.

"Well, yes, it's entirely possible that we're lost," Nigel replied, hitting the group with the full force of his snaggle-toothed smile. I wasn't sure if English charm was exactly the right tone to take with these particular folks, but Nigel burbled on anyway. "We're looking for the Voice of Colockum Ridge."

"You got business with Roger?"

"It's more like we're longtime listeners, first-time visitors," Nigel chirped. "Comrades in the fight for freedom."

"Comrades," the wiry man said.

"Or partners?" Nigel's voice went up a full octave. "I thought comrades because we like Russian strongmen, don't we? But look, it doesn't matter. Let's go with listeners. For a long time, we've listened. And now we're here to help," he paused, as if deciding on a cause. "Here to help, ehm, take down that peckerwood."

"Nigel!" I yelped, and he looked over at me and hunched his thin shoulders toward his ears. "Just making conversation. Feel free to join in anytime."

The woman laughed and turned to motion her friends toward us. I took off my glasses and swept my hair forward so it covered some of my face. "Keep the engine running," I whispered to Nigel. "Obviously," he spat back at me, voice dripping with disgust.

"We've got somebody all the way from," the woman turned back to Nigel, "What is it? England?" Nigel nodded enthusiastically. "He's going to tell us all about that peckerwood from Seattle. What he knows about him, anyway."

"Oh, I know quite a lot," Nigel said, cutting his eyes toward me. "I know where he lives."

"Yeah, everyone knows that," one of the ex-jocks said disgustedly.

"Oh," Nigel said. "Well, that's good surveillance on your part, then. And I know good surveillance, due to my professional background." When none of the patriots took the bait, Nigel leaned out of the window and crooked a long finger toward them. "Ex-MI5," he whispered.

"What?" the wiry man said.

"For Go . . . goodness sake, Nigel," I hissed. "They don't stream BritBox out here."

"His Majesty's Secret Service?" Nigel tried.

The woman took a step back and cocked her head at a skeptical angle. "Right," she said. "Well, nothing else going on tonight anyway." She glanced at her friends, and all four moved close to the Dreadnought. I couldn't see if the men carried guns too, but out here with this bunch? It was a good bet.

The leader stuck her face through the open window until it was only inches from Nigel's. "Know this, 007. We're fighting for our way of life out here and we're serious as cancer. Trust me when I say you better not be coming up on the property without a good reason." I heard a metallic tap, the gun against the SUV's door. "Now tell us about The Peckerwood."

"Well," Nigel nervously began, "It always pays to know your target's habits and beliefs, and he has some strange ones. You already know about the woodpeckers?"

The group nodded.

"He also has a thing for craft ales. That is, posh beer. Not like what men usually drink." He shifted his shoulders toward the woman. "Pardon me, miss. I mean to say he drinks the beer of the elites, unlike, the beer of the—" Nigel glanced at me. "The beer of, ehm, the beer of the patriots."

I made a low growling sound, and Nigel cut me the side eye once more.

"He hangs out at that pathetic pub in La Likt," Nigel continued, and I wondered again if he really thought carrying on with this particular line of bull would ingratiate us with Thorp's crew. "You know the place: the one with the nine-dollar beers and the pointy-head name, Cenozoic Brewing. You can find him there almost any time you want."

This time Penny growled.

"We should probably get going," I said.

"Don't be in a hurry now that you're here," said the woman. "Hangs out at the tavern in La Likt, then. What else?"

"Well," Nigel nervously tapped out a rhythm on the steering wheel with his pointer fingers. "He reads a lot. Seems unnaturally interested in wildfires, so you have to ask yourself, 'Why is that?'"

The woman's eyes met mine. "Why is that?" she slowly repeated, but Nigel was on a roll.

"He also reads a lot about Charles Darwin, in point of fact." One of the ex-football players shrugged while his friend said in a low voice, "The king guy?"

"Evolution," Nigel pronounced. "He thinks man is descended directly from apes. That's why he loves to chat with that chimpanzee woman. You won't find either of them at church on Sunday mornings."

One of the ex-jocks kissed his hand then pointed skyward.

"Really should go now," I said. My voice shook—with fear, yes, but also with anger. I cleared my throat loudly in an effort to regain my always elusive cool.

"And the toilets," Nigel was warming to his subject. "He wants us all to use toilets when we're out enjoying the wilderness, correct? Hunting and fishing and, you know, shooting at the road signs with deer on them?" He gave the group a wide-eyed stare. "Toilets! Out where man has always gone free! And whose taxes are going to pay for those, do you suppose?"

The men nodded vigorously. The woman actually spat, and I couldn't contain myself any longer.

"It's because of the water quality! You want to fish in water that's contaminated with E coli? You want to drink it?"

"Beth," Nigel warned.

"Because good luck with your digestive system if you do!" I could feel the adrenalin surge out through my limbs, setting my fingers and toes to tingling. Who did these bozos think they were, screwing up the local watersheds and then calling my husband a peckerwood?

"You want to talk about going freely?" I raved on. "About loosening regulation? You'll find out just what that means if you drink out of the La Likt River!"

Nigel eased the Dreadnought into reverse.

"But there's a simple solution!" I was nowhere near finished telling these small-town tyrants where to get off, and I bent over Nigel the better to get in my enemies' faces. "Latrines!" I shouted at them. "Nothing fancy, just a place to stow your stool that's away from your water source! How hard is that for you to understand? Okay, maybe Nathan's a little overboard on the subject, but he only has public health in mind. Your health, and maybe the health of the watersheds. I remember when we were on our honeymoon—"

"There it is," Nigel said grimly, removing his foot from the brake so that the Dreadnought began to roll backward slowly.

"Honeymoon," said the woman. "I thought that bitch looked familiar. She's the fake news wife!"

Nigel stomped on the gas, and the SUV spun gravel. The front end waggled wildly as we careened backward toward the chainlink fence and out to the washboard road. Penny was barking furiously now, and I could see one of the figures on the ground in front of the house. Had we hit one of Thorp's acolytes?

Nigel took the washboard so fast I could swear we were skimming over the tops of the ridges, barely touching the dirt below. That was, until I heard part of the exhaust system drop off with a loud clang. It bounced into the dried grass lining the road, and I hoped the heat it held wouldn't spark another fire.

Nigel checked the rearview mirror. "Now this is surprising," he said, yelling to be heard above the staccato bounce of the

Dreadnought's loose contents, including the crate-less Penny. "They're not following us."

"They don't have to," I said, my voice jittering in time with the ridges in the road. "They know where to find us."

Chapter 6

Nathan takes a hike

Again, my new blog post draft would require edits. Some trimming. Perhaps some toning down. But after saving the draft and scurrying around the cabin to pack for my hike, I thought it was headed in the right direction.

[DRAFT BLOG POST #20]

The Straight Poop
OFFICIAL BLOG OF THE DRAKE WATER QUALITY PROJECT

Being a Good Neighbor to Fire

Fire is a natural phenomenon that sustains biodiversity in many stunning western landscapes. It's essential for the survival of species such as, to pick just one, that magnificent denizen of the burn zone, the three-toed (aka black-backed) woodpecker. (See Blog Post #19: At Home in the Burned Forest.)

Yes, wildfires can cause havoc for humans. Homes, lives, and local economies can be lost. Smoke-filled air is unhealthy and unsightly. As witnessed in our own community recently, the consequences can be tragic.

But if we could somehow eliminate wildfire completely, the long-term consequences for our natural environment would be unacceptable. Entire complex plant communities would vanish, replaced by unhealthy, cramped, unsustainable monocultures.

The ultimate outcome—as we've been finding out, in fact, in the wake of our century-long experiment in total fire suppression—would be megafires feeding on overgrown forests, causing even more havoc for society.

So how do we balance the need for healthy fire with our need for safety? How can we become a good neighbor to fire?

Good fences may keep your neighbor Bob happy and in his place. But a good cedar fence around your big rural home in the Cascades will likely go up like a Roman candle and bounce sparks to your roof before you can locate your Go Bag.

Here's the most important thing we can do now: stop building our homes in the middle of the forest, which is just asking for trouble. Even housing developments on the suburban edge, in the so-called wildland-urban interface (the WUI, or "whooee") are playing with fire. Those neighborhoods are, to put it bluntly, meant to burn. Anybody who builds there, and the municipalities that allow the developments as well as the insurance companies that underwrite them, should not be surprised at the consequences. Neither should they come to the federal government looking for bailouts when the inevitable occurs.

In the upper Sahaptin, too many of our forested hills and ridges are now sprouting homes on two- and five-acre parcels smack in the middle of highly flammable mixed conifer forests. Prescribed burns and clearing decrease only a tiny fraction of the threat. At Skylandia, the mega-lodges sit like kindling in the shadows of drought-stressed Ponderosa pines. Their lush golf courses and private firefighting force will be no match for the wind-whipped fire certain to visit them someday. And above La Likt today, snaking amidst the thicket of second-growth dog-hair pines and firs, new roads are being laid for a vast development of over two thousand homes.

These new homes should not be built. Those houses already in the path of fire should not be insured. Only common sense financial disincentives based on fire science will turn the tide away from future conflagrations.

As part of this course correction, we as a community also need to begin a serious discussion about whether or not these homes in the forest merit protection from local, state, and national firefighters when the fires come. Lives must be saved, of course. But properties? Homes built where they should not be? It's worth discussing.

[WRAP UP. SHORTEN! BRING FULL CIRCLE BY DISCUSSING MERITS OF CONCENTRATING HOUSING IN CITIES AND DENSER SUBURBS? WHY NOT TOWNHOMES IN DOWNTOWN LA LIKT (COULD INCLUDE PARKING FOR SNOWMOBILES, MOTORBIKES, OVERSIZED TRUCKS? TOO FAR-FETCHED?) BENEFIT OF REDUCING THE CLIMATE FOOTPRINT? TOO MUCH? BENEFITS OF WALKABILITY? WRONG AUDIENCE?]

"I don't disagree with all you're saying in your blog, Nathan," said Twyla, breathing hard behind me as we climbed straight up the north ridge trail above Johnny Boy Creek. "I just have little faith that people will suddenly, you know, stop building in the middle of the friggin' gorgeous forest."

"It's aspirational, I know," I replied. "Just planting a seed."

"Not sure the soil is ready for your seed."

Whatever the odds on my seed, my final edit on the blog post would have to wait because Twyla and I were headed up the Icicle Creek drainage to look for woodpeckers. The original plan was a group hike, but that plan fell apart. I'd texted Twyla at 5 a.m..

You up?

Yep.

Early bird!

Always do my rosary and Wordle before coffee.

Nice.

Hot already in the apartment! Got the fan blowing all over me on the bed.

So, Dave had to cancel. Brewery emergency.

I heard. Beth is going to Seattle, can't make it.

O no! Glenn can't come either. School project.

Reschedule?

Hmmm.

Kinda your call.

Smoke looks better today. I'm still up for it if you are.

So, just the two of us.

We had almost broken out of the thick cover of hemlock and firs when I saw him.

"There he is," I said, pointing to a little brown bird that was singing its heart out. The trail here was so steep we could direct our binoculars straight over to the droopy top of an 80-foot hemlock without craning our necks. There, the world's most ethereal songster filled the forest with its long, sad notes. A rare treat to see a hermit thrush, normally so secretive, perched up so high in the sunlight.

"Yeah," I said as we resumed the climb, "the blog. I could tone it down a bit."

"Don't want to make enemies," Twyla said. "Counterproductive, you know?"

I was puffing hard again so just managed a grunt. "Huh. Yeah."

"And actually," she continued, "I mean I've never been to your cabin, but aren't you, technically, in the whooee?"

"Kind of grandfathered in. Built in 1902."

"But yeah, like, I guess here's what I really want to know about you and fire," she went on. "Have you ever tried other ways to get your point across? More direct action?"

"Like what?"

"I don't know. Words alone don't change minds these days. Print, blog, radio, whatever. We're all preaching to the converted. But something like your High Country Crapper Project. That's direct action. Not just talk."

"True," I agreed. "I yapped about that for years before doing anything."

I needed a few steps before I could catch my breath to say more. Twyla must be, what? With a son almost out of high school, about 40? Whatever, she was in better shape than me.

"Until I retired . . . no time . . . to actually grow the water quality project."

We finally broke out of the green forest cover and moved into the most recent burn zone. Shiny black husks of tree trunks stretched for miles to the north—a ghost army of charcoal skeletons. They marched all the way up the ridge. Our progress from here was slow because we had to step over many of the blackened trees that lay across the fading trail.

"Wow, this is surreal," Twyla said, pausing to take in the beautiful hellscape. She produced a blue polka dot bandana from the pocket of her hiking shorts and mopped at the sweat on her brow and neck. Then she reached down with the damp bandana to try to erase the jagged stripes of black ash on her inner thighs.

"So tell me this, Nathan Drake," she said, looking up and catching me staring at her thighs, which had been only partially restored to milkiness. She swatted me with the bandana before continuing. "What would actually change minds around here about fire?"

"Nothing like a good old-fashioned catastrophe to hit the reset," I said automatically. My days working in water quality for the City of Seattle had taught me that sewage spills and citywide backups were the surest trigger-puller for investments in aging infrastructure. Three-inch thick reports on corrosion and flow rates just didn't capture the public imagination like rafts of stinking dookies floating in the local canal.

"So, maybe it's time for a High Country Inferno Project, right?" she said, punctuating her idea with a loud "Ha!"

An inferno project? Was she joking? I couldn't tell. "Kind of living that right now, aren't we?" I said, then turned to lead the way on.

"Maybe somebody beat you to it," she called brightly from behind me, punctuating the comment with a weird half chuckle, half snort.

We were in the heart of the burn now, the original trail just a memory. Over the years, winds had toppled a good portion of the charred trees. We stepped over their blackened corpses and struggled through the thick growth of fireweed, manzanita, and lupine—all the flowers, berries, and seedpods of those post-fire invaders crackling under our feet in their late summer desiccation. Twyla's legs must be taking a beating from all this undergrowth, I thought. They would certainly need the bandana treatment again, I saw as I helped her over some of the larger downed trees.

As we continued uphill, I kept thinking about Twyla's odd comment. "Maybe somebody beat you to it," she had said. I knew what she was getting at, but I couldn't shake off the strange way she said it. A disturbing image gradually took shape in my mind and then began to play like a video clip on repeat. It went like this: Twyla is alone up the Stafford Creek drainage, bare knees dug into a patch of dry grass, shoulders hunched in concentration over a tricked-out pack of matches; the pack suddenly sparks to life and she is bounding down the trail toward her beat-up Toyota van, ponytail flapping, that odd chuckle-snort echoing through the forest.

"Nathan," she whispered from behind me, her lips suddenly an inch from my ear.

We stopped.

Her hand was on my shoulder, breasts pressing against my back. Technically, they pressed against my daypack. But I was aware of the pressure.

A hollow, methodical pecking resounded from the nearby stand of blackened snags.

She wrapped her free arm around me and pointed straight at a dead tree just 15 feet away.

"Oh my God," we both whispered, our damp bodies pressed together, not wanting the moment to end.

Seconds later, shoulder to shoulder, our binoculars rose in unison to focus on the fire-adapted specialist with three toes and a jet black back.

*****

It was Twyla's idea to check out the spot where the Happy Mountain fire started. The exact location and cause still weren't nailed down. Muriel had been strangely tight-lipped with details when Beth called her after the community meeting. But most locals I talked to thought the valley floor over the ridge from the Novak cabin and the chimp sanctuary was most likely ground zero. It was just a short detour from our drive back to La Likt after our successful day of birding, so here we were. Even though I was ready for a nap.

About half-way up the road, we met a white Tesla headed down the hill toward La Likt.

"That looks like Thorp's fire investigator," I said as both vehicles slowed to pass on the narrow road. "The one at the meeting, with the goatee and the suit. That's him, right?"

"Huh," said Twyla. "Still checking out the scene, I guess."

I rolled down my window and stuck my arm out, palm forward. He stopped, and the Tesla's tinted window slid down to reveal the natty dresser himself.

"Dr. Heath, I presume," I said, smiling across the foot-wide gap between our windows. "We saw you at the community meeting."

"I was there," he said, looking over my bony forearm to focus on the occupant of the Subaru's passenger seat. "I certainly remember seeing you at the meeting."

"Hey there," said Twyla, now leaning forward, her hair suddenly liberated from her braid and hanging in unruly waves over the center console and my right leg. "I was impressed with your findings. About the couple from Seattle in the van?"

A self-satisfied smile appeared on his face. "Most cases are exactly as they appear," he said. "Just requires a little shoe leather. A little time in the lab. The occasional bit of court testimony and explication."

"Ah yes," I said. "Well, nice work. And what are you finding up the valley here? Is lightning still the prime suspect in the Happy Mountain fire?"

He refused to take his eyes off Twyla. "I shouldn't say anything until the investigation is complete. But, off the record, just between the two of us, I'd say the odds favor some unfortunate conjunction of that nasty power line with one of those poorly tended trees."

"Well, that's interesting," I said.

"Wow, your job must be so cool," said Twyla, now practically sitting in my lap as she leaned toward the Tesla driver.

"We're just out doing some birding today," I said, trying to look straight ahead through the windshield but seeing only Twyla's abundant locks and smelling orange blossoms. I willed myself to concentrate on the conversation. "Thought we'd scout the fringe of the burn zone."

"And who are you working for, exactly?" Twyla asked.

"Oh, I'm an independent investigator," he replied.

"Yes, but, really, who's paying you?" Twyla persisted. "Like, an insurance company? A private homeowner? It's all so interesting."

"I've got many, many different clients," he demurred, finally peeling his eyes off Twyla to dreamily scan the road in front of him. "Fire is affecting more of us these days. I just try to make sense of it, apply science and the law."

"Isn't Thorp your client?" I asked. "Why is he so interested in the Happy Mountain fire and the La Likt River complex?"

He pointed ahead, tapped his steering wheel twice, and said, "Better get out of the road. I think someone may be coming our way. Nice chatting. Be careful up there."

With a spray of gravel, the Tesla whisked him off.

Twyla turned her head, which still hovered very near mine, to watch the departing Tesla. "A low clearance vehicle like that has no business on these rutted roads," I said, watching the sedan's dust cloud fade in my rearview.

Farther up the road, I parked the Subaru in a pullout alongside a white Nissan truck. We expected a few fire-fighting rigs up here doing mop-up operations—we even thought they might kick us out of the area—but this dinky truck clearly was not official. A magnetic sign was stuck, cockeyed, on the driver's side door. It read "Hector Hernandez: Yakima Tree Trim & Removal Company." An extension ladder held together with duct tape was roped to the truck's rack. I got out of the Subaru and took a look in the truck's dented bed: a five-gallon can for gasoline and two chain saws, along with a litter of crushed Coke cans and a beat-up lunch cooler covered with stickers from some place called Tamales Don Chayo.

Twyla and I began wandering up the road. It was hot in the full sun. The hillside to the south was crispy black with wisps of smoke still curling from the ashes. The creek below carried a surprising amount of water. I spotted an American dipper, a comically chubby bird with a stub of a tail, doing bouncy knee-bends on the rocks at the creek's edge.

A row of high metal towers, each bearing three cross arms, ran alongside the road. At the end of each cross arm, a short stack of white ceramic bracelets hung down to grip a high voltage cable. The towers and their power lines ran for another mile or so uphill before angling off across the creek and climbing the opposite unburned hillside. Over the hills they went, from the spine of dams along the Columbia River to power-hungry Seattle. I could imagine the six power lines drooping and rising in parallel the whole way, crackling like a giant exposed nerve across the landscape.

"You must've been up here lots of times," said Twyla.

"Mostly to check out raptors," I said. "Up near the ridge above the old orchards."

"How do you think the fire started?" she asked.

"Well, Heath may be right. A downed power line is usually the prime suspect. But it could have been lots of things." I scanned the high blue sky. "Could even have been a hawk landing the wrong way on the lines. It's possible they can get zapped and cause a fire." I looked over at her. A fine sheen of sweat had formed at the base of her throat. "Lots of things are possible," I said. "What do you think?"

"No idea. Heath is sure full of himself, though." She stopped abruptly, gathered her hair over one shoulder, and started to weave it back into a rough approximation of a braid. Then, the job nearly done, she looked at the burnt hillside and asked, "So would you call this one of your healthy fires?"

I stared at the road leading uphill and sighed. I was too tired and hot to make a case that the bleak terrain above us was the result of a good fire. As I tried to form an answer, a black-and-white dog, about the size of a Jack Russell Terrier but likely without the pedigree, rounded the bend in the road ahead. He caught sight of us, paused briefly, then made a beeline for us as fast as his short legs would allow.

"Aww," said Twyla. "Where'd you come from, sweetie pie?"

About 20 feet away from us the dog braked hard. He stared at the still-cooing Twyla, gave his jaunty tail a tentative wave, and then looked back up the road where he'd come from. He stopped his panting long enough to issue one sharp bark. Now we all looked back up the road. Nothing.

"He looks well cared for," I said. "Nice collar. With the truck, you think?"

"But where are they?" Twyla asked. "Who knows how long that's been parked there?"

After a few minutes of waiting, I extracted a short length of nylon cord from my daypack. Twyla coaxed the pup close enough to attach the cord to his collar, and we led him under a pine near the creek to get out of the baking sun. Seated in the shade of the tree, Twyla and I took turns scratching our new friend behind his ears. His panting slowed and he eagerly lapped up the water that I poured from my plastic bottle into its blue lid. After about ten minutes, the pooch finally plopped down in the short grass, occasionally lifting his head to look up or down the road. In unspoken agreement, Twyla and I also lay back and waited for whatever would happen next.

I drifted in and out of sleep. Whenever I woke, I gazed up through bushy clusters of long needles into the painfully blue sky. So nice to get a break from smoke. I kept expecting to hear someone calling for their dog, but the woods were stubbornly quiet. The dog licked pensively at my forearm, and I thought about how Beth and I found Penny on the Pacific Crest Trail. How we searched for the owners. Why we decided to keep her. She's such a good dog, I thought, despite her recent actions. Twyla snored lightly.

I woke to a melancholy whistling coming from the direction of the creek. Was it a lullaby? A hymn? Or was it just the murmur of water playing on my tired mind? I checked my watch. The three of us had dozed for about 20 minutes. The dog was now standing, head cocked. I moved toward the creek bank, where the whistling seemed louder. I bellowed out a "hello?" and heard thrashing across the stream, behind the willow thickets.

The little dog began yapping. He tugged on the leash and Twyla, standing now, let it go. She looked only half awake.

"What is it?" she yelled above the dog's racket.

Before I could answer, a dark-haired girl, probably somewhere in her early teens, jogged around the bend in the road above us. She paused briefly, just as the dog had, and fixed Twyla and me with a disbelieving stare. Then she looked back up the road. Coming behind her was a middle-aged man—dad, I figured. He didn't stop. Instead, he hurried toward the girl, phone in one hand and a can of Coke in the other. The two of them exchanged a few words in Spanish as they made for their dog.

"Emmet! Ven aqui." the girl said. The dog ran toward her, my make-shift leash dragging, and then hopped excitedly at her feet. The girl removed the cord and clipped a proper leash on the happy little fellow. Now that she was closer, I could see she was older than I first assumed. Maybe 16 or 17. She wore a pair of baggy men's jeans that could use a washing and her flip flops were held together by duct tape. Her dad—if he was her dad—was older than I'd first assumed too, and dressed similarly to the girl.

"Hello," I belted out, my hand held absurdly high in a we-come-in-peace greeting. Even I realized that this gesture was overcompensating for my sad monolingual state. The girl hugged her dog and stared at me. I glanced over at Twyla, wondering if she could help.

At her usual volume, she said, "What a cute little dog." She smiled first at the girl, then at the man. "Did he run ahead of you to get back to the truck?"

The man and the girl looked at each other, their expressions serious. Dad issued the communique. "Somebody tried to take him," he said.

"What?" Twyla and I said in unison.

The girl seemed to be scrutinizing me, checking out my face and clothes. "Weird guy," she finally said. "My papa was up the hill inspecting the power lines. I was waiting with Emmet. This creepy guy was whistling and Emmet took off after him, barking. The guy scooped him up and ran across the creek." She hugged the little dog even tighter and took a deep breath. "We've been looking for him for an hour." Her eyes were moist. "Thank you for finding him."

"Look there," said her father, pointing down the road. A sporty-looking sedan pulled out from a smaller side road and sped downhill in a cloud of dust.

"Maybe that's your weird guy," said Twyla. She turned back to the father and said, "I'm so glad you have your Emmet back, although Nathan and I were becoming quite fond of him."

"Were you checking out the fire?" I asked.

"Yes," said the father. "I have a day off today. Very bad fires all over."

"We're birdwatchers" I explained, grabbing my binoculars to make the point visual. "Today, we saw a black-backed—"

The girl cut me off. "My papa leads the crew that cuts trees along the power lines for oop."

"Oop?" I asked.

"E-W-P," she spelled. "Eastern Washington Power."

"What a hard job," sighed Twyla, "and an important one."

"Yes, it's very hard work," said the man. Hector Hernandez, if the truck's sign was right. He grimaced, and his sun-creased face seemed to break into a dozen discrete regions—rutted middle forehead, squinting left eye, deep rivulets framing his mouth. He looked at his daughter and shrugged.

"We're taking photos of the places the crew cleared," the girl said, her rush of words addressed to Twyla. "The power company says my father's crew missed some trees. They say the trees fell on the power lines and caused that big fire."

"Seems like the power company would be responsible in the end," Twyla said, her tone reassuring.

"My papa and his guys are subcontractors," the girl quickly replied. "Actually, a subcontractor for the subcontractor. Work for hire. The power company needs someone to blame."

"I'm sorry to hear all this," said Twyla. "You know, I'm a reporter for the North Sahaptin County Courier and I'd love to talk with you both some more."

The girl's eyes were on her dog. "We live in Yakima," she said, as if that ruled out anything good from ever happening.

"I can talk with you anytime. Tomorrow maybe? If I get your phone number?"

The girl assessed Twyla—including a long look at her stylish lightweight hiking boots—before trading her dog's leash for her father's phone. She swiftly sent her contact information to Twyla's phone. "Lindsey Hernandez," Twyla said, gazing at the screen. She smiled and handed the girl her business card.

The girl regarded it with deep curiosity before sticking it in her back pocket. Then, eyes back on the phone, she pulled up some photos and showed Twyla the device. "Intact power lines," Twyla said, her eyes meeting mine. "Straight-as-an-arrow clear cuts on either side. Plenty of clearance."

"Papa says, where they found the broken power line? The trees were all good. The line's repaired now, but E.W.P. says a tree knocked it down."

"They're liars," said her father, but there was no real heat behind his words. He sighed heavily.

"This morning they threatened us," the girl said. She addressed her father in Spanish, tapped at the phone, and then twisted the screen up into my face. The text message there carried a Sahaptin County area code:

We know you started the Happy Mountain fire.
Go back to Mexico or you and your family die.

"Who sent you this?" I asked.

The girl shrugged.

"Not E.W.P., huh, Lindsey?" said Twyla. She, turned to me and lowered her voice. "Sound familiar? From the community meeting?"

Apparently seeing no advantage in chatting up some birdwatchers, Mr. Hernandez had checked out of our conversation, but Lindsey was full of righteous fury. "In the sixties, Papa's father came up here every year to pick apples," she said. "My grandfather. Right here in this valley." She stamped a flip-flopped foot in the ashy dust. "Abuelito crossed for good in 1980, and Papa was born in Yakima in '81. He had to go back to Mexico for a while after my grandparents died, but he came back, met Mom, and they had me and my sister."

The girl looked angrily at the text message. "He's a citizen," she practically screamed. "Started Yakima Tree Trim 12 years ago. Big crew. Does the work nobody else wants. Too hard for them."

"Show them the building," the girl's father said, pointing to the phone. After a rapid string of Spanish and more pointing and nodding, he repeated, "Show them the building where the big fire started."

The girl shrugged and told us, "Papa thinks the fire started in the old Bountiful warehouse just up the road here." She tapped back into the phone's photo app and showed us an image of a cinder block building about the size of a basketball court. The red paint had almost completely faded off the cement blocks, but traces of the elegant Bountiful logo—orchards, stream, mountain—were visible.

"That's just a quarter mile up the road," I said. "Been out of commission for decades."

The girl's father nodded to Lindsey and pointed at us.

The girl shrugged and told him, "Go ahead and tell them if you want, Papa."

"I was near the warehouse two weeks ago when my crew was trimming. I saw someone messing with the power line nearby. But not E.W.P. Not Bonneville Power. This guy was actually climbing the tower. He had a red truck, a big Ford 350."

He paused, then seemed to come to a decision. "I'm pretty sure they were stealing power for something they had going in the warehouse," he said. "Some kind of grow operation."

The girl jumped in. "But tell them the whole story. So, when Papa drove down to see what was going on, the guy pulled a gun on him. Told him it was private property."

"Yeah, and so I left pretty fast," her father said, nodding his head vigorously. "I'm pretty sure they're growing marijuana. All locked up, but it smelled funny outside."

*****

After parting with the Hernandez family we continued our walk up the dirt road past a long-abandoned orchard—the decrepit apple trees full of yellow-rumped warblers and mountain chickadees—to the old fruit warehouse.

The low-ceilinged cinderblock building sat in a small clearing at the base of the burned hillside. You can find variations on these structures for fruit storage all over central Washington. The wood ones from the early 1900s were partially underground. The thick-walled cinderblock and concrete structures came along mid-20th century. The new ones are all gigantic and refrigerated, near rail lines.

"This place probably shut down around the time Hector's father picked apples here," I told Twyla as we walked around the warehouse. "All the orchards got big. Consolidated. Shifted to Yakima, Chelan, Okanogan County. Now they're down along the Columbia in Douglas and Grant counties, too."

A couple of showboating western tanagers high in a nearby pine distracted me. When I caught up with Twyla near the back of the warehouse, she was studying an ancient electrical panel box hanging on the wall next to the oversized roller door. The box was streaked with black marks, possibly burns. Before I knew it, she had popped open the warped and rusted gray cover and was examining the array of wires, insulators, and switches inside.

"Interesting," she said, pulling out her phone and taking pictures.

"Some of that looks new," I said, pointing to some connector gizmos with fresh plastic and shiny bolts.

"Yeah," she said. "The parts that aren't burnt out."

"Could be Hector is right," I said. "Someone tapping the line for a grow operation?"

We turned and noted the nearest electrical tower, just ten yards away. It all looked normal to me, but what did I know about power lines? And why did Twyla seem to know so much?

Twyla took another photo and mumbled, "The only bountiful things up here are those kilowatts."

"Take a look," I said, peeling off a dollar-sized strip of white paint from the boards surrounding the electrical box. Underneath the new paint, the board was scorched black. "Looks like fresh primer."

She moved in to fleck off a few more skins of paint. The eaves above the panel had received the same hasty paint job.

As we studied the warehouse, a red pickup truck appeared on the road seemingly out of nowhere—the rattling engine and eruption of dust suddenly just there, in front of the warehouse, as if parachuted out of the blue sky like an Apollo space capsule of my youth.

"Where the hell did that come from?" Twyla yelped, grabbing my shoulder and pushing me against the warehouse wall. We heard the diesel engine rev high before dying. A door slammed and footsteps crunched on the gravel, headed toward us. Twyla pushed me around the corner of the warehouse in the opposite direction. Once out of sight, we peeked around the corner of the building and saw a guy in khaki work clothes and a white hardhat. He plunked a cardboard box beneath the electrical panel, pulled a can from the box, popped it open, and started slathering gray paint on the box and the surrounding wood frame.

"He hasn't seen us," I whispered in Twyla's ear. She grabbed my hand and led me back around the warehouse to the red truck, a brand new Ford 350, no company logo on the door, with heavy-duty metal work boxes hanging off the sides.

"Give a hey-ho if you see him coming back," whispered Twyla, backing away from me and aiming her phone at the truck. She took a few photos, then tiptoed to the pickup's far side, crouching down casually and reaching under the passenger-side door, as if checking for damage or taking a sample. Or looking for a secret compartment.

"Nothing," she reported. "Let's get out of sight." She took my hand again and towed me at high speed up the road away from the warehouse. We stopped behind a cluster of small pines and wild azalea that the fire had spared.

Painting evidently complete, the man opened the electrical panel box and used a wrench to remove a few connectors. He threw them in the cardboard box along with the paint supplies, then moved up the hill to the nearest tower. There, to my surprise, he hefted a heavy coil of rope out of the burned grass. The rope was partially burned, and I could see a few carabiner clips and a mesh harness attached. He carried both rope and cardboard box to the truck and tossed them in the bed. Then he made a full tour of the exterior of the warehouse, returning to his truck with a handful of little metal clips, which made pinging noises when he tossed them into the bed. He wiped his hands together, got in the truck, made it roar, spun it around, and headed down the hill.

"Okay, that was interesting," I said as we emerged from our hiding place. We made another complete circumnavigation of the warehouse, ending up at a metal side door.

"Somebody else has been here recently," Twyla said, bending to pick up a few cigarette butts. She dropped several into a small baggie that appeared from the pocket of her shorts.

I turned the knob and gave the door a cursory shoulder bump. To my surprise it popped open and a rush of cool air poured over me. Twyla squeezed past me in a flash. A moment later, I followed her inside.

Beams of light entered the warehouse through pinholes in the roof. As our eyes adjusted to the dim interior, we could make out three rows of metal racks running down the center of the warehouse. They were empty.

"These are new, too," I said, aiming my phone's flashlight on the racks. "I got some just like this at the Home Depot in Ellensburg."

Small coils of electrical wire, broken glass, and bits of metal and plastic connectors lay scattered over the concrete floor. Two clear plastic barrels, half-filled with water, sat on a long countertop that ran the length of the warehouse. Several blue tarps were folded and stacked on a table.

Near the back corner of the room, hanging from the wall opposite the electrical panel outside, a tangle of thick wires had been crudely hacked off just above the floor. Scanning the ceiling, I thought some of the roof beams looked charred, but it was too dark to see for certain.

"Hey," Twyla said.

An empty cigarette package—white and gold with the letters "MS" in black and red—lay crumpled at her feet. She pocketed her phone and crouched to pick it up.

"Hmmm," she mused, still crouching, holding the pack at eye level to examine it in a dusty shaft of light. "Who smokes Italian cigarettes?"

Chapter 7

Nigel thinks like a monkey

Every time I see Mary Beth in action, I wonder how she ever became a reporter.

"The evacuation area is closed, Nigel," she told me in that school teacher tone of hers. "If the families who lost houses can't go in, I don't know how we can justify gawking at the ruins, even if we could get past the sheriff."

She was standing in the narrow slot of her kitchen, setting out slices of bread two by two on paper towels spread across the counter. It was time for daily sandwich assembly: one for her husband, one for herself, one for Cassie, two for James, two for me, and six quick ones as a special treat for the chimps. Her trainers squeaked as she pivoted on the scarred kitchen floor and in one fluid motion yanked open the fridge. After a moment, she extracted a jar. I groaned. Peanut butter today.

"And why would we even consider taking Penny?" she continued, waving a butter knife coated in Jif toward the pine table where I sat with my mug of tea. "She's not search and rescue trained simply because she sat in on one informational meeting."

God, it was all so tiresome. The sooner I got her out of the way of the story, the better.

"Quite right, quite right," I chirped back at her, teacher's best boy. Behind me, James Novak moaned loudly and shifted deeper into the grotty cushions of the ancient settee. With a good deal too much dramatic flourish, he pulled over his head a hideous, orange and pink knit comforter—an "afghan," Beth had informed me, made by her gran's own hands, no less.

"That's why you'll be going over to the city to interview that couple The Doppelgänger was on about at the community meeting," I explained to her. "The couple pulled over for, what was it? Dragging a chain? From their Mercedes-Benz Sprinter van?"

I'd only recently learned that dragging a chain from one's Mercedes-Benz Sprinter van could lead to quite a bit of trouble. Sparks might fly when chain struck pavement. Miles of fires might be kindled as one drove, oblivious to the havoc. It was positively thrilling to learn how many creative ways Americans could start a conflagration.

"I don't know," Beth said, annoying me anew. "Is it really worth going to see them in person? What's wrong with the phone?" She'd stuffed a sandwich into her canvas school bag along with her notebook and pens and now she stopped, red apple in hand, while she considered abandoning the interview.

I stifled the urge to shake her. Instead, I smiled. "Your charm, Mary Beth, is much more potent in person. We'll need that to convince them to talk. And let's not forget your rigorous eye for detail, which is lost to us on the phone." I eyed the various portable lunch items she now pulled out of a large plastic bin stored on top of the refrigerator. "I'd like M&Ms today," I said.

"Okay, I guess," she said truculently, throwing a "fun pack" into a rumpled paper sack inscribed with my name in bleeding red ink. Mary Beth had us all recycling and reusing furiously these days, and I'd toted the same sack several days in a row now. The brown paper was as soft and furred as a granny's cheek. Beth cinched up her school bag, then headed toward the splintered front door before remembering it was boarded up, the result of the attack on her peckerwood of a husband.

"Why can't we just get things fixed, like normal people," she muttered, spinning on her heel and heading for the back door. She passed the sofa holding the human-shaped lump that was James Novak and sighed. "See you this evening, Nigel. Take good care of Penny."

Once the generic hum of Beth's Subaru had faded, I headed for Penny's ramshackle kennel, which was appended to the massive garage under construction near the cabin. It was by far the most ambitious, modern, and structurally sound edifice on the entire Drake estate, and it seemed no closer to completion than the last time I had seen it almost two years ago.

Inside, the chimps were finishing up their morning hooting. I could hear Cassie working with them. "You got the eye of the tiger," she bawled, her brassy voice wandering freely over the musical scale. "And it's hoot, hoot, hoot, hoot, hooty-hoot!"

I quickened my pace toward the dog's pen. Penny looked at me quizzically as I snapped the lead onto her collar.

"They underestimate you, Penny," I said as the dog leapt into the Dreadnought's first row of rear passenger seats. "Let's go get little Brooklyn."

Open beside me on the front seat was The Peckerwood's second best map of the region, plus his guidebook to edible plants, a laminated sheet comparing the tracks of various animals, and a squat booklet covered in plastic titled "Avalanche Safety." I wasn't completely sure which of these I might need, but I felt better knowing I was prepared for several types of wilderness emergency.

"The idea now," I told Penny, "is to think like a monkey."

Since arriving in La Likt, I'd had several informative conversations with Cassie Chimpanzee about the hooting primates now inhabiting The Peckerwood's half-finished garage. According to Cassie, the chimps were vocalizing so much because they were anxious due to the fire, as were we all. But they'd been made even more nervous by the fact that their leader, Holly Chimpanzee, hadn't made the trip down the mountain with them.

Holly was out in the wild, and so was little Brooklyn. Each chat with Cassie made me more confident that the two of them had escaped the flames together.

In the wild, it's not likely Holly would have been a leader, Cassie told me. That position almost always goes to a male, and please don't let's waste time with comparisons to human behavior. We all know what we know. Plus, one tries not to anthropomorphize, but with a chimp as smart as Holly that was a challenge.

"I'm teaching her American Sign Language," Cassie told me, tears springing to her eyes. "She knows 56 words. She loves playing in her wading pool and sitting in the sun, eating fruit. And cowboy boots! She can't get enough of them! If you wear cowboy boots near her, look out, she might just take them right off your feet. Chimps are strong—about four times stronger than a human that's roughly the same size."

How could such an extraordinary animal neglect to save a child lost in the middle of a burning forest?

"I guess it's possible," Cassie said dubiously when I presented my theory to her. "Holly had four babies during her years in research, so maybe if she found Brooklyn, and if Brooklyn was willing, Holly might have picked her up." She'd paused, then added, "Of course, adult chimpanzees have also been known to eat human babies."

"But that's very rare," I told Penny as we trundled off down the highway toward Cassie's property. "Not well documented."

Well before reaching the sheriff's blockade at the fire line, we took a hard right off the pavement and started up a pot-holed forest road. After a mile or so, we left the dark green canopy behind and crossed into the ashy gray moonscape of the fire zone. Burnt rocks that seemed to have somehow floated to the surface of the ash jabbed at our tires as we crept along. It was slow going, but according to

The Peckerwood's map, the track would take us several miles in the direction of the chimp sanctuary.

"Did you know chimps can reach speeds up to 25 miles per hour when running?" I asked Penny. "But in the wild, they rarely travel more than two to ten kilometers from home. That's why we'll begin our search at Cassie's sanctuary."

In another mile, our progress was stopped dead by a large boulder that evidently had become dislodged from the hillside above. It now sat, sunk in the gray-white ash of the road surface, blocking our way.

"No matter, Penny. We'll walk."

Walking in the forest isn't my strength at the best of times. Walking in the recently burned forest was torture, like hobbling along a rocky beach at high tide in a dense fog. I stumbled over the charred ground, my foot finding every soft divot that once held roots which were now turned to ebony twigs. Anything that might provide shade had been consumed, and the sun burned through the smoky air, casting everything in the sepia light of a William Blake scene of hell. Ash rose in gritty puffs with our every step. A twisted ankle and sunstroke seemed the best I could possibly hope for. Penny sneezed repeatedly as she pulled me along, lifting her paws high off the powdery surface.

But she kept moving as if on a planned route, and I was glad one of us felt so confident about our direction. She even emitted little whimpers of excitement as she hopped ahead of me. Perhaps she'd been here before on one of the interminable hikes Mary Beth and her husband consider pleasurable. At any rate, after a particularly unpleasant 45 minutes, we reached the top of what I later deduced was La Likt Ridge. Below us the remains of a small village smoldered beneath a layer of smoke.

"The La Likt Ridge Townhomes?" I asked Penny. She pulled on her lead and we started down the slope toward the ruins.

The condominium complex seemed to have once contained three or four dozen two-story homes arranged in blocks on either side of a large swimming pool. The pool was studded with blackened bits of household goods. Still, its aqua waters glinted invitingly amid the gray and white landscape. Penny headed straight for it, placing all four feet on the second step of the graduated stairs leading to the shallow end.

"Bloody hell, Penny. Did we burn your feet?" I felt an emotion for which I can find no description other than sympathy.

The scene around the pool was confusing. On one side, plastic chaise lounges stood neatly stacked against a masonry wall, waiting for sunbathers. On the other, their mates were blackened lumps of resin. Most of the condominium blocks—I counted evidence of ten in all—were heaps of gray rubble with twisted pieces of metal, bits of crockery, and perhaps a book or a boot sticking out like evidence of a lost tribe. Strips of bright green grass marked where one ruined building left off and another began.

Two of the buildings—the blocks closest to the access road—still seemed more or less intact. And from the furthest building, we heard barking.

"Somebody's pet seems to have made it," I told Penny, who, ears canted forward and nose in the smoky breeze, began howling as if in response. An identical howl sliced through the abandoned townhomes, and a dog who looked like a larger version of Penny bounded out of the furthest unharmed building and streaked across the grass toward us.

"Do you two know each other?" I asked the dogs as, sniffing, whining, and wagging their whip-like tails, they greeted one another. The bigger dog wore a collar, and after some coaxing, I was able to get close enough to read the silver tag that hung around his neck. "Big Red," it said, followed by a ten-digit American telephone number. I felt something engraved on the back of the tag, so I turned it over and saw the words, "Pete Novak."

Brooklyn's grandfather?

"Brooklyn!" I yelled, and the dogs helpfully began barking as we hastily made our way toward the building from which Big Red had emerged. The three of us were so loud that it took me a moment to hear a sound above our own efforts—the now-familiar pant-hoot of a chimpanzee in distress.

"Holly?"

We reached an open door and Red and Penny bounded through. I was not far behind.

At the top of the stairs the space widened into a living room-dining room combination, kitchen off the front. There, the cabinets were flung wide open, as was the double-door refrigerator. Bits of food were strewn across the counter and the floor—bread wrapped in ripped plastic, an unopened tin of tuna next to a jar of pickles with missing lid, plastic bottles of water at various stages of consumption, and a torn box of something called "Lucky Charms." At first, I was not entirely sure of the use for the charms, but apparently it was food. That is, if one believed the cartoon leprechaun jigging across the carton under the words, "It's magically delicious!"

In the living room, across from a television measuring at least 52 inches, a chimpanzee squatted atop a brown leather sofa, deeply denting the cushions. The chimp's lips were curled back in a warning grimace. In one hand she held a blackened banana. In the crook of her opposite arm, she held a little girl who appeared to have been interrupted while enjoying a toaster pastry. A red, jammy substance oozed between her tiny fingers.

"I knew it!" I crowed to the assembled group. "Holly, I knew you had her! What a good chimp! Really, what a marvelous monkey you are."

Holly bared her sharp teeth in response, and I tried not to think about what Cassie had told me regarding the strength of chimpanzees. I also recalled that Cassie had impressed upon me the differences between the great apes, which included chimpanzees, and monkeys, which did not. Perhaps I had insulted Holly? No matter. I couldn't retreat now.

But as much as I was prepared to hold my position, I was loathe to step up to the chimp and snatch the child from her. It was at this impasse that I slipped out my phone and recorded the video that was soon to make me famous. With the jam-covered babe still under one arm, Holly charged just as I tapped "record." I scampered around the counter that separated the living area from the kitchen, and, thankfully, Holly suddenly stopped. She panted at me rather chillingly, then retreated to her spot on the sofa. The standoff that followed lasted a tense 51 seconds, as I attempted to reason with the chimp.

"Holly," I said firmly, "let Brooklyn go. I mean, good job. It's simply a top-rate job you've done. But now it's time to let Brooklyn go back to her, ehm, people." I thought of the lumpish James, currently living on Beth's settee, and just for a moment, I considered whether my efforts here were truly in the best interests of the child.

Holly pant-hooted, dropped her banana, and picked up a fancy-tooled cowboy boot that sat next to her on the sofa. She lofted it toward my head, and I dropped into a crouch as the boot flew past and connected behind me, sending a wooden figurine of a bear holding a fishing rod crashing off a side table.

"All right," I said, slowly rising to a standing position. "Don't get your knickers in a twist."

I understood the chimp was protective of the little girl. But if Holly thought I was going to lose this story—a story that would bury my colleagues, at this moment sunning themselves in Malibu, as well as Des Conner, sunning himself elsewhere—well. She wasn't as intelligent as Cassie thought.

While I considered my next move, Red trotted lazily toward the sofa. He had the same soulful golden eyes Penny possessed, and now he seemed to use them to connect with Holly. The two gazed at each other for a long moment, then Red licked Brooklyn's face, causing her to let out a delighted giggle. Holly looked at the girl, then at Red, and finally over at me. The grimace evaporated from her face, replaced by a look of great melancholy. She sighed, and still holding the girl in her left arm, she raised her right hand. Slowly, repeatedly, she moved her fingers in a pattern unknown to me.

"Are you signing?" I asked her. "Holly, is that American Sign Language? Because, you see, I don't sign myself. But I promise you this, Holly Chimpanzee: I will take Brooklyn back to her people. And I will do the same for Red. And Penny."

I was rather proud of this speech, but the chimp remained unmoved. "And you, too, Holly," I quickly added. "Cassie is very worried about you. Cassie, and the rest of your community. You must come with us too."

I stared into Holly's eyes and felt a connection with the chimp far deeper than I feel with most humans. I attempted a sort of sign language of my own devising, pointing toward the exit then giving Holly a thumbs up. "Holly," I said. "Let's go home."

Holly gave me an appraising stare. I haven't felt so closely evaluated since grammar school examinations. She sighed once more, and then set Brooklyn down beside Red. The dog's floppy ear in her sticky hand, the little girl toddled toward me.

*****

Brooklyn, Red, Penny, and I came upon the Forest Service assessment crew no more than a half-mile down the road to La Likt.

Sent into the fire zone to make a record of property damage, they were not happy to see us.

"Yes, but you don't understand," I said as they threatened me with all manner of grave punishment for entering the evacuation zone. "This is Brooklyn Novak, the little girl lost on the night of the fire. Tell them, Brooklyn."

"Booklyn," the little girl dutifully responded.

"She was up in the La Likt Ridge Townhomes, or what's left of them," I continued. "Holly—the chimpanzee, you know—is still up there. We couldn't get her to come with us."

"Holly," Brooklyn said.

This confused the firefighters well enough that they left off trying to handcuff me and instead loaded the four of us into their vehicle. We were, they assured me, not out of the woods. In fact, they fumed, we were bound for the county seat of government and an audience with the most powerful authorities. I perched Brooklyn atop my lap and told them that was perfectly fine, as long as wherever we ended up had decent WiFi. "Heroic reporter discovers toddler in care of wild chimpanzee"—I was already writing the story in my head.

Suddenly, the driver braked hard.

"Shit," he said. "Look at that."

Above the burned treetops, in the direction of La Likt, rose the familiar mushroom shape of a pyrocumulus cloud.

Chapter 8

Nathan remembers Red Top

Again La Likt suffocated under a blanket of smoke. The brown layer of combusted pine filled the Upper Sahaptin from Ellensburg to Snoqualmie Pass.

"Just one silver lining to all this," chuckled the old cowboy standing next to me in the lobby of the La Likt post office. Side by side, we stood at the table by the expansive bay window and sorted mail from our P.O. boxes. The garbage receptacle situated between us received the lion's share of our correspondence. I threw our ads from Technical Mountain Supply and Pacific Northwest Ballet on top of his from Mid-County Plow and Ellensburg Yarn Corner.

"Excuse me?" I asked, unsure whether I'd heard him right. Dripping with sweat, I'd just hopped off my bike and was anxious to get back to our cabin to see if Penny had found her way home.

"All this smoke," he explained, turning his entire body in my direction as if his neck no longer functioned. "Silver lining is that the temperature drops by fifteen degrees when the sun doesn't make it through."

Oh. The guy was just being nice. Noticed my bike, the sweat.

"Ha," I said, finally meeting his eyes, which were the same faded blue as his denim jeans. A heavy gold wedding band glowed on his left hand, the one he used to toss his junk mail. "I bet your wife appreciates that kind of optimistic outlook," I said.

"She did," he replied, one eyebrow flinching up before he managed a crooked smile. "Except for every March when I bet a hundred bucks on the Mariners to go all the way."

"Ha," I said again, lamely covering my gaffe. We turned back to our mail. The sweat still dripped from my nose onto my pile.

My Mayo Clinic newsletter landed atop his McCoy gun catalog. My glossy Skylandia brochure—"Your Legacy in the Woods"—twirled down to cover his AARP Medicare Supplement Plan mailer.

"Peoh Point," I heard him pronounce.

"Come again?"

He gazed south out of the window and across main street to the promontory that looms over La Likt. The treeless volcanic bluff is the most recognizable geologic feature in the upper valley. Now, it was just barely visible through the thick haze.

"Different every time I look at it," he said, not moving, only one official-looking envelope now squared up before him on the table. "Like those haystacks the French guy painted a hundred times. Monet? Manee? Different in every season. Every time of day. Yellows. Pinks. Browns. And now in the goddamn smoke!"

I joined him in regarding the familiar rock. To my eye, it resembled nothing as much as the Titanic foundering in a sea of Sahaptin smoke.

Time to go home. Time to find Penny.

I tried to limit my breathing while peddling back up to the cabin. That only made things worse, and in the end I needed to suck in several deep lungfuls of that nasty air to avoid passing out. Cooling off inside the cabin, I felt certain I was forgetting something. Possibly I was addled from smoke. Beth, I remembered, was off somewhere with Nigel. Or, wasn't she already on her way to Seattle for Paula's wake? She had the Subaru, I remembered that. Where was James? And Cassie? Too much going on. I jogged from the cabin to the garage, again trying and failing to hold my breath before reaching the outbuilding's side door.

Was all this smoke due to a flare-up of the La Likt River fires? A change in wind direction pushing the smoke toward us? A dying breeze that failed to push it away? Or maybe was it from some other fire entirely? The acrid taste at the back of my throat suggested a new source. Now I was a smoke connoisseur?

Sirens whined in the distance, but when didn't they lately? I hadn't had time to check the latest news, and I needed to get back on my bike to look for Penny. When I got home from my hike with Twyla, my pooch wasn't in her pen. I figured she'd escaped again, and I feared for Mr. Clucker.

But first, I needed to check on the chimps.

The garage was dark inside. On a hot day like this, I thought the chimps might prefer the shadows so I didn't flick on the overhead LEDs. Or maybe that was my preference—a way to hide from the smoke. Or the chimps. In any case, I fumbled in the dark, topping off water stations and adding figs, zucchini, and seed bars to the trays on each cage. Perhaps due to the smoke or heat, the whole group was lethargic. They were unusually silent as I made my rounds.

As I said, I wasn't comfortable around the chimps. Beth says my fascination with biology is intellectual rather than due to any love of animals or plants. And it's true, I prefer pondering life's origin and complexity in books and ideas—ideally at the micro or molecular level or on the geologic timeframe—rather than wrangling with actual squishy life. So while proximity to my closest living relative in the animal kingdom was fascinating on one level, on several other levels it creeped me out. I felt guilty about the research these animals had endured and responsible for their vanishing jungle habitat. I felt privileged to enjoy a longer and far more interesting life than they did. Even though I personally had nothing to do with creating any of my human advantages and luxuries—books, television, antibiotics, shoes, lights, pistachio ice cream—they were still mine for the asking. It was my stupid luck and none of their own.

Complicity for their continuing bondage also weighed on me, as did responsibility for the smoke seeping into their lungs at this very moment. Embarrassingly enough, I had also recently recognized in myself a certain degree of outright fear of these garage dwellers. Bred no doubt by my too-frequent viewing of the Planet of the Apes movies while in grade school, I could not escape the feeling that these hairy creatures would soon turn the tables and mount horses to hunt me down as I ran naked through the fields.

For all these tangled and absurd reasons, I felt harshly judged by these six strangers—silent, watching, not quite animals but not quite human—as I moved from cage to cage accomplishing my chores.

Finally done, I lowered myself onto the concrete floor and wrapped my arms around my knees. Worn out by the day, and also abashed by my utter lack of resemblance to Jane Goodall, I heaved a sigh and mopped my sweating head with my shirt sleeve. Immediately, Freddy, the ten-year-old chimp, moved forward in his cage, picked a green zucchini off his tray and offered it to me through the bars. I leaned forward and took it. "Thank you, Freddy," I said, genuinely touched.

In the adjoining cage, Freddy's younger brother Samuel began hooting. He rattled the bars of his cage in frustration. Like the other chimps, he was not used to being caged for so many days in a row. Life at Cassie's sanctuary included free-ranging in a generously sized pasture. Freddy sized up his brother and turned back to me. We shared a long look into each other's eyes. His were black and unblinking. What on earth could he be thinking? Samuel, still riled up, flung an old carrot, hitting me on the shoulder. Freddy glanced again at Samuel, then returned his black eyes to me and cocked his head as if to say, "Can you believe this guy?" Or perhaps, "I will tear you apart given the first chance."

Samuel gave a long hoot and sprang onto the wooden stool inside his cage. He crouched on the stool, displaying his teeth in a taut grimace. He tilted his head back to examine the garage rafters, then sniffed the air and swept the room with his eyes for points of escape.

Clearly, he felt trapped and wanted out of here. He radiated fear, rocking atop his chair, looking wildly left, right, up.

And that's the image that unlocked the flood. No sooner had Samuel's frightened pose on his chair reached my retina than a shiver passed through my entire body and I immediately reclaimed the memory—so vivid, so complete, how had I suppressed all this?—of my night with The Doppelgänger on Red Top.

*****

It happened about ten years ago, before Beth and I bought our cabin. We both were still working full-time in Seattle, so we came up on weekends, staying with Paula and Pete at their Happy Mountain place as we started to explore and fall in love with the upper Sahaptin Valley.

In the spring that year Beth and I along with a dozen other eager volunteers completed training to work as fire spotters at the Red Top lookout above town. We were awarded a coveted multi-day assignment chiefly because Muriel was our good friend, but also because she knew that we had the skills to construct a new cedar privy for the lookout. So, a win-win.

Red Top, like most of the classic lookouts in northwest forests, was no longer strictly necessary, what with the proliferation of cameras, satellite infrared, drones, and cell phones in the forest. Technology and crowd sourcing were replacing the old-school fire lookouts with their binoculars, maps, and radios. But Red Top was Muriel's baby. She led the restoration effort and she made sure select citizens were able to spend a few nights every year up at elevation 5,300 feet where, even if their fire-spotting was subpar, they could enjoy spectacular sunrises, sunsets, and star shows. During the day, Red Top offered 360-degree views of the Stuart Range and Teanaway

Ridge as well as the Chelan and Entiat mountains and even Mount Rainier and Mount Adams.

The Forest Service saw the volunteer program as a P.R. win. For Muriel it was a labor of love. Her final admonition on the last day of training, delivered with a jokey but—you could not mistake it—a deadly serious undertone, was, "Don't burn down my lookout."

As it turned out, when our assigned days came up Beth had to work all weekend. So I went by myself. No big deal. These were the formative days of my water quality project, but I'd already built dozens of toilets on my own. And frankly, a few days playing the part of the lonely fire spotter seemed highly romantic.

The Doppelgänger showed up at dusk on my second day on Red Top. Throughout that July afternoon, the scattered clouds had multiplied and then coalesced into a towering bank of thunderheads. But just before sunset, all that drama and potential energy in the sky simply vanished. As if a plug had been pulled, the sharp black and white edges of the clouds swiftly dissolved into a blur of reds and oranges. I was enjoying a beer and watching the wreck of the sunset from inside my aerie when I saw him limping along the ridge toward the lookout. He stopped near the base of the stairs and slid off his backpack. I heard boots on the steps and then a knock on the door.

Gazing out the glass panes, I had the singular shock of looking into my own face. Like a reflection, there were my own gaunt cheekbones and the hooded brow over my deep-set eyes. The subtle beaky tilt of the nose. There, the broad Irish forehead barely contained under a Mariner's cap. The scruffy salt-and-pepper beard. Even the jagged blue veins at the temples and, how perfect, a white dab of sunscreen stuck in the curl at the top of an ear. The tan Eddie Bauer shirt hung on bony shoulders above a flat chest, as if on a wire hanger. All the similarities were striking, familiar, almost too intimate. But of course, I'm recollecting this years later. In that moment on Red Top, I'm sure it was less the particulars and more the essence of that face, some gestalt of the total physiognomy, that set my facial recognition software ablaze. No doubt, those face-selective neurons in my brain—exquisitely sensitive and usually employed in everyday tasks like picking out my wife in the produce aisle or conjuring up the name of the actor stepping off the steam-belching train in *Shadow of a Doubt*—that's Joseph Cotton!—were totally confused and screaming "Hey, that's me there. What the hell? That's me over there! Red alert! Red Alert!" These days, a similar short-circuiting often occurs when I'm shaving and see, peering back at me in the mirror, the skull and doleful, sometimes playful, eyes of my dear departed uncle Bob. But I've grown accustomed to that milder form of facial self confusion. It's not unwelcome.

Anyway, The Doppelgänger. In the few seconds I took to survey and recognize my own face, my visitor apparently was managing the selfsame process. I opened the door and we stood for an additional second or two in silence, as if to verify what we had both just seen. But there was not to be any acknowledgment of this bizarre reunification. Our resemblance, our twin-hood, was never mentioned, not then or in the days to come.

"Hey," he said, letting his eyes break away and roam the interior of the lookout, "Cool place. Sorry to bother you, but I twisted my ankle coming through the agate beds over there on the ridge." He looked over his left shoulder and gestured vaguely to the east. Then his eyes were back on me. "Wonder if you might have an elastic bandage. Or even, like, a crutch."

I invited him in. Part of the lookout gig was to serve the hiking public in the event of just such accidents. My visitor's ankle was already badly swollen. I found a heavy duty ankle brace in the medical kit and gave him some ibuprofen. The brace was a good fit, but even a few ginger steps had him wincing in pain. I invited him to spend the night so he could rest and elevate the ankle instead of continuing down to the trailhead. He ended up staying that night, and the following day and night as well.

He was good company and helpful, hobbling around to lend a hand with crapper construction. We had many common interests in science and the environment, similar low-key dispositions, and eerily identical ways of clearing our throats and fiddling with our baseball caps. The talk flowed easily, even when the differences between us became clear. Over morning coffee on the second day of his visit I learned it'd been a rough year for my doppelgänger. He'd lost his business—he worked as an electrician—and soon after that, he and his wife divorced and she got custody of their kid. Finally, the bank foreclosed on his home—200 acres up Taneum Creek. These days, he told me, he rented an apartment between La Likt and Patrick and cobbled together jobs as a handyman, mostly at the big houses in Skylandia.

He blamed it all on the Great Recession.

"I got screwed," he told me. "No bailout for guys like me when real estate collapsed. And no government benefits to legitimate small businesses getting undercut by immigrant labor. Just more tax bills for me."

His views weren't so unusual around here. And I was not unsympathetic to his plight. The swipe at immigrants definitely could be debated, but I wasn't hitting a guy when he was down—especially after he told me he didn't see his young son much since his ex-wife had taken the boy over the mountains to live with her parents.

The best I could do for him, I figured, was to listen and distract him from his troubles. That morning we spent a couple of hours going over the lookout's equipment. He was fascinated, as were most visitors, by the 1934 Osborne Firefinder, which sat at the very heart of the lookout like a brass gear within a Swiss watch. Perfectly level and lightly oiled, the Osborne relied on the delicate and carefully plumbed horsehairs in its sights to pinpoint the center of a fire and translate that into an exact position on a map. In our training session, Muriel had told the tale of a colleague's husband who had snapped one of the crosshairs. The couple was now divorced, Muriel reported, holding us under her stern gaze as if any other outcome would be preposterous.

After playing with the Osborne we scanned the mountainsides for smoke with our binoculars. We radioed in a small plume I spotted near Teanaway Butte, but it turned out to be from a prescribed burn. We decided another wispy cloud was actually a water dog—water vapor rising after the previous day's brief rain shower. Then we descended the stairs and finished digging the hole I'd started the day before.

Our conversation bounced easily from topic to topic. We covered the evolution of songbirds, the geology of the Cascades and the Columbia Basin, and the agenda of the political action group Stop Population. That led us to immigration policy, pandemics, shrinking glaciers and aquifers, climate change, and our favorite camping spots. We took up the varied merits of the Seahawks and the 49ers, Darwin and Dawkins, RNA and DNA, composting toilets, the Mariners pitching rotation, the origins of religion, and the rye bread at local bakeries. And we finished, as I recall, with a discussion of electric cars, solar cars, our father's old cars, and the many potential applications of light-weight drones. In other words, the same repertoire of topics that flutter through my monkey mind every day.

For the life of me, I can't remember The Doppelgänger's name now—maybe it will come to me. But I do recall very clearly that we also talked about the need to reintroduce fire into the landscape and limit development in fire-prone areas. It was toward the end of the day, after we'd screwed together the little cedar box, added the seat and lid, and secured it to the platform above our very professional hole. Again that afternoon the thunderheads had built in the southeast, and now those dark skyscrapers were drifting up the Sahaptin Valley toward Red Top.

"You think we'll get some storms tonight?" he asked, as we climbed the steps to the lookout.

"Could be," I said. "And maybe, if we're lucky, a few lightning strikes and some good fires, right?"

That's when the discussion turned serious. I ranted my usual rants about how some big fires need to run their course and how some homes just shouldn't be built in the forest. He mostly listened and, by the time we'd finished our first beers and the sky had darkened ominously above us, he mostly agreed with me.

"Sure it's inconvenient for plenty of homeowners who choose to build way out in the forest," I remember saying, "but actions have consequences, you know?" And, probably because I had just popped open a second beer, I added something melodramatic along the lines of, "Sorry, but man shall not have dominion over the fishes and birds and every living thing. Fire will have dominion. At least for the next 30 years or so."

At one point, he looked at me a long while and then absentmindedly lifted the bill of his Mariners cap before snugging it back into position. "Nathan," he finally said, "I guess you're right. We can't just cut our way out of this. For one thing, there's no market for these dog-hair trees. The small diameter stuff just doesn't price out."

I followed his gaze across the carpet of forest spreading in all directions to the horizons. "Can you imagine the Forest Service budget required to thin the millions of acres that need it?" I asked him.

"The risk to homes out there is so extreme," he said. "It's like building in a flood zone."

"Exactly," I said. "And you know where that leaves us?"

He rejiggered his cap and waited.

"Right here," I said, wafting my hand toward the forests above La Likt. "It's just waiting to happen. Ripe to burn. All those planned new homes above La Likt? All the Rocky Ridge development along the river? They should not be built. It's unsustainable."

"It's idiotic," he agreed. "Bad enough to build a home that's four or five thousand square feet. That kind of greedy consumption needs to stop. Fewer people. Lower consumption per person."

The Doppelgänger was definitely speaking my language there. We both seemed to have enough self awareness to realize that our shared impulse to stop building in the forests was not just about fire safety. It also betrayed our shared disgust with the relentless growth in human population and the typical consumption habits of humans. You know us. We're the guys who fire off terse comments on news stories saying the only real solution to the intractable problem— climate, species loss, disease, war, housing, famine, socioeconomic inequities, whatever the crisis of the day—was reducing the human population.

"People say Ehrlich was wrong with his book The Population Bomb in '68," I said. "I say he was early."

"You should check out the Stop Population group, Nathan," he said. "SP is full of latter day Ehrlichsonians. Some interesting action committees."

"Yeah, I'm finished with my research phase," I said. "Time for me to actually do something."

Apparently in full agreement, buzzing from the beer, we gazed out at the Yakima River Valley and the ridge line above La Likt.

"You've walked those hills," I said, eventually. "You know the forest is kindling. Ready to go up."

"Yeah," he said, "I can't wait."

I may not remember everything about that night, but I'm certain those were his exact words.

After a dinner of spaghetti and sourdough, we played a few rounds of Scrabble. The wind buffeted the lookout and fat raindrops pelted the metal roof. There was no colorful sunset, only a rapidly lowering black curtain. We were asleep by ten.

The first soft illuminations flashed way out near Ellensburg, 25 miles away. Those puffs of light were attended moments later by low rolling rumbles. I sat up in my sleeping bag for a few minutes to observe the distant light show. An hour or so later, I was jolted awake by a burst of the purest white light and felt against my chest a near simultaneous explosion. Hail clattered like BBs off the roof, windows, and deck. Seconds later, the next bolt of hyper-illumination revealed that The Doppelgänger and I were both out of our bags, standing in our boxers and T-shirts, staring at each other. The hair on his head stood upright. A buzzing filled the air. My skin tingled.

"Get on the chairs," I yelled to my double. Muriel had taught us how to avoid electrocution in a lightning storm by perching on our chairs after capping their legs with old-fashioned glass insulators—the types you still see on some rural telephone poles. We struggled to find the insulators and jigger them on our chair legs. The next flashbulb on my retina left an image of my guest crouched on his chair, knees akimbo, looking up—to the roof? to the sky?—and, judging from his expression, praying to what we had both agreed only hours earlier was a nonexistent God. We rode the chairs through the heart of the lightning storm—another 45 minutes of pure terror. The closest I've ever been to death.

When the storm had passed, I balanced on the chair for another 15 minutes just to be sure it was over before crawling back into my bag to try to sleep. I'm sure The Doppelgänger saw me, but neither of us said a word. Hours later, I woke and saw that he was still crouched on the chair—a lot like Samuel Chimpanzee—still raising his anxious face to the sky, which was now calm and illuminated only by the moon peeping through clouds in the west.

That was the last I saw of him.

Just before sunrise, I was dipping in and out of a long dream involving Muriel and me stalling out in a small plane, or some type of flying office, that was taking off from a postage-stamp mountain airstrip. At that sickening moment when forward momentum stopped and gravity began to pull us down, I jerked and gasped. At that half-waking shudder, I felt immense relief that it was just a dream—that I was alive. Drifting back to a state of half-dreaming, I swear I felt lips pressing on my cheek and heard The Doppelgänger say, "We'll be okay, Nathan."

Dream or not, he was gone when I got up at sunrise. The whole thing was highly weird. I knew I had not imagined the entire doppelgänger experience. But, really, no one else could confirm he was there, could they? Or maybe I was just letting my imagination run wild with the whole doppelgänger-ness of the guy. And the Irish goodbye, that odd kiss, what was all that about? Maybe the dreaminess of the situation, the strange ending, is why my brain eventually parked the entire episode in the Trash file.

Even back then, though, I was ready to let the whole thing go, work my final day at Red Top without burning down Muriel's lookout, and return to my lovely wife in Seattle. And I was well on my way to that happy resolution, sipping my coffee, recalling the violent thunderstorm, and scanning the western hills with my binoculars, when an old-fashioned alarm clock began trilling somewhere inside the lookout. I found the tiny wind-up Timex smack in the middle of the central map table. I picked it up and pushed in the metal stem to silence the thing. A yellow Post-it Note had been placed under the clock. Written in an angular hand was the current time along with a set of exact longitude and latitude coordinates. I checked the coordinates on the map—it was west of

Red Top on the flank of Malcolm Mountain. Over the ridge from La Likt. When I trained my binoculars in the direction of those coordinates, I saw a healthy plume of smoke rising. I spun around and prepared to aim the Osborne's sighting ring on the fire but was confused to find that the Firefinder's vertical and horizontal horsehairs were already perfectly aligned over the smoke rising through the forest. I called it in and the Forest Service crew out of La Likt leapt on it.

I had prevented a major lightning-caused fire. I had saved the Middle Fork of the Teanaway.

Or, quite possibly, I had created a monster.

*****

Both Samuel and Freddy now peered at me thoughtfully as if they were attorneys, fraternal law partners in adjoining cages, simply waiting for the man sitting cross-legged on the garage floor to finish his deposition. Samuel still crouched atop his chair, but he was calm. Freddy rested his chin on his interlaced fingers. He looked frankly concerned for my ability to stand trial.

And for good reason. Because I was now shivering in a cold sweat on that concrete floor, wondering if my big talk about the stupidity of building in the overgrown forest had somehow flipped a switch in The Doppelgänger, turning him into an eco-terrorist, an anti-growth activist, a killer of my wife's best friend.

A siren chirped on the street. Just one yelped note, trailing quickly, then silence again, like a friendly tap of the car horn to announce a visitor. All three of us—Freddy, Samuel, and I—turned our heads toward the street and waited in the dark, as if for a judge to re-enter the courtroom.

Chapter 9

Beth takes a sentimental journey

Walt and Eleanor Lundquist were the ideal western Washington couple, circa 1992. He was a former software developer, one of the original Microsoft millionaires who joined the revolution early on. She taught Spanish at the local community college, shepherding generations of Seattle teenagers to Oaxaca each spring. They hiked, they biked, they skied. They spent weekends climbing Mt. Rainier and Mt. Adams and raised three extremely successful children. Now in retirement, they spent their leisure time birdwatching from their fully outfitted Mercedes van—and quietly funded a half-dozen local environmental groups.

"What we don't do is set fires," Walt Lundquist told me as I settled into a deck chair at their modest Madison Park home. "Not even a campfire in established campgrounds. We hate the smoke."

Walt and Eleanor lived in something of a Seattle specialty: a three bedroom, two bath mid-century rancher. It seemed the definition of middle class living—until you walked from the entry hall to the living room and ran smack into a jaw-dropping view of the Cascades over glittering Lake Washington. It's astounding to think that until relatively recently the families of public school teachers and Boeing machinists lived with views like this.

Now, of course, little houses like these are rapidly being replaced by luxury townhomes. Advocates who want to abolish single-family zoning say this will provide much-needed housing for everyone. We'll see. For now, Walt and Eleanor still had their view.

They also still had a subscription to the local daily newspaper, which is how I got past their front door in the first place. When I rang the bell and gave them my name—they were still listed in the phone book—they recalled my byline from years before, congratulated me on my new gig with the international press, and invited me in.

"It's true that we were pulled over by a state trooper when we were coming home from Colockum last time," Eleanor said once we were seated on the deck with cans of store-brand sparkling water bubbling before us. "And it's true there was a chain attached to the undercarriage of the van. And it was striking the pavement. The trooper saw it spark."

"But we've never had a tow-chain on the van," Walt insisted. "We've never towed anything with the van. We don't even have a hitch."

"Were you camping up on the La Likt River?" I asked.

No," said Walt. "We just made a quick stop there on our way home. Someone told us there were black swifts near the waterfalls." He shook his head. "If it was Vaux swifts we wouldn't necessarily go out of our way. But black swifts? That's special."

I nodded. Vaux's are fairly common around La Likt in summer. Black swifts are a much better get, bird-wise.

"Eleanor, you mentioned you were headed home to Seattle when you got pulled over," I said. "But where were you coming from? Did I hear you say Colockum?"

"Yes. We own some property on Colockum Ridge. It used to be planted in timothy hay, but we're trying to restore it for wildlife habitat now," she said. "We go up there maybe once a month to see how the project is coming along, and this time we took a detour through La Likt on the way home because of the swifts."

"Colockum Ridge, huh?" I said. "Do you know Roger Thorp?"

Walt rolled his eyes toward the sky, which seemed all the brighter blue to me after having spent the last several days under ash fall. "Boy, do we ever know Roger Thorp," he said. "He owns the property adjoining ours on Colockum Ridge. And he's let us know that he doesn't appreciate our land being taken out of hay production."

"Why would he care about that?" I asked.

"Maybe he used to ride motorcycles up there, or maybe he hunted the fields after harvest—I don't know," said Walt. "But some of the locals aren't happy we don't allow motorized vehicles or guns on the property anymore."

"Did you know Thorp is something of a media celebrity?" I said. "He's one of the people pushing the idea that the La Likt River fires started with your dragging chain."

Walt and Eleanor looked at each other in surprise. "Does he write for the paper out there?" Walt asked.

"He has a radio program on a local station, and he distributes a videocast of the show online," I told them. "You know how conservative Sahaptin County can be. He plays to that audience. People who don't share his opinions are pretty much at fault for everything that happens around La Likt. Like if there's a fire, maybe somebody from the west side had a chain dragging on their van."

Walt shook his head. "I was born here, and I know there's always been a rivalry between the west side and the east side of the state," he said. "Liberal Seattle versus conservative Spokane. UW Huskies versus Washington State Cougars. But when did it get so bad that both sides are ready to jump all over each other, no questions asked?"

The three of us gazed east toward the crest and all that lay beyond it.

"One thing that really mystifies me about that chain," Walt said. "I swear it wasn't there when we stopped at the gas station on the

Bullfrog roundabout, before we got on I-90 to go home." He turned to his wife. "Remember, Ellie? You got out to use the restroom, and I took a good look at the rig, just to make sure we had everything stowed. I sure didn't see a chain. If I had, I wouldn't have left it hanging."

"Still, somehow there was a chain," Eleanor said. "We saw it when the trooper pulled us over."

"But even if there was a chain," Walt continued, "And even if it was hitting the pavement, why wouldn't we have noticed it earlier? It was a little smoky out, yes, but it was getting dark by the time we left the waterfalls. Wouldn't someone have seen sparks?"

He took a sip from his can. "There was a guy in a Camaro, one of the newish ones, kind of banged up. He was tailgating us all the way down from the lake. One time I looked up at the rear view and caught him throwing garbage out of his window."

Walt squinted across the lake again. "I usually try to get out of the way of guys in a hurry like that. So, I pulled over to let him pass, which he did. But he must have turned off somewhere up ahead of us —maybe he waited for us to pass by—because five minutes later he was back on our bumper."

He turned and looked at me, brow furrowed. "If there were sparks coming from our van, why didn't he see them and stop us?"

*****

Back in the Subaru, I could hardly wait to give Muriel my hot tip on the La Likt River fires. Not only was the Camaro driver a potential person of interest, but if Walt really had checked out his rig at the gas station, maybe there'd be security camera footage. I pulled up contacts on my phone and tapped my friend's name, then waited impatiently for her to answer—which she did, on the fifth ring.

"What do you need?" she barked at me.

"Hi! It's me!" Her cold tone startled me, and I found myself nervously stumbling over my words. "Sorry—you know who it is. I just wanted to tell you something I learned from the Lundquists."

"What the hell, Beth? You're talking to the Lundquists? They're part of an active investigation."

"Well, Je . . . Jiminy Crickets, Muriel. It's not illegal to talk to them." I knew my friend was under a lot of pressure at work. Still, I wasn't used to having to defend myself to her.

She paused for a few seconds, then heaved an exasperated sigh.

"Where's Nigel?"

"I don't know," I said. "I'm on my own, just running down a few leads on the fires."

"Well, stop it!" Muriel demanded. "We don't need your help with this, Beth. In fact, you and Nigel are now officially hampering our investigation. When we have something to report, we'll hold a press conference, which you'll be welcome to attend, just like any other member of the media."

After a stunned second, I said, "Muriel, did something happen?"

"Geez, Beth, no! That's what I've been saying! When we have something for you, we'll let you know. Until then, stay out of our way."

"Okay," I said in a small voice.

"Was there something else you were calling about?" she asked.

"Um," I replied. "No. Nothing special. Sorry to bother you."

I punched the red button on my phone and spent a half-minute looking at its blank screen. Then I started the car and headed for my next appointment.

*****

Kelly Rafferty was a friend of a friend—a kind-hearted insurance adjuster who'd agreed to meet me so I could get some background on the industry and its reaction to our state's increasing wildfire risk. I spotted her as soon as I walked through the doors of the downtown coffee house we'd chosen as a meeting place. Like almost everyone else in the shop, she sat behind the glowing screen of a laptop. But her elbows were planted on either side of the keyboard, and she held her face in her hands, her fingers shoved up under her glasses and pressing gently on her eyelids.

"It's been a tough day," she said once we'd settled down with our skinny lattes. "They're all tough days."

"What happened?" I asked.

"Oh, just the usual set of calamities," she replied. "Only multiplied by ten. Plus, I'm starting to get reports out of the Happy Mountain fire. The first claims are coming in."

"Will everyone be covered?"

Kelly shrugged. "It's more and more common for people not to carry fire insurance. Some can't afford the premiums—they've been doubling and sometimes tripling every year. And lots of people had their coverage cancelled after that bad fire season we had. Remember that? A big part of Pateros was destroyed, and then a few years later it was Malden. The companies don't want to take on any more risk, so if you live in a rural area, it's hard to find someone to insure your home against fire."

"Has it gotten worse lately?"

Kelly blew on her latte and nodded. "I've been an adjuster for 22 years, and I can tell you climate change has made my job a lot harder. A lot sadder, too. Every year it seems like we have more severe storms, mudslides, flooding. Tornados where there never were tornados before. And, of course, a lot more wildfire."

"Does anyone stand to profit from wildfires?" I asked. "Would anyone have a motive for starting one?"

Kelly pursed her lips and gazed at a poster on the wall opposite us: rows of glossy coffee plants with pickers moving through them, baskets full of beans at their hips. The people in the posters weren't smiling. "That would be awfully dangerous, not to mention evil," she said. "But yes, there are people who profit from fire, although that's a long way from having the motivation to start one."

"Like who?" I asked.

"Oh, maybe the construction industry," she said. "If people have the resources and the will to build back after a fire. Sometimes contractors from out of state will temporarily relocate to a burned-out town to get in on the uptick in business."

I scribbled "construction" in my notebook.

"And private firefighting companies," she continued. "If people are wealthy enough, they can hire their own firefighters to protect their homes, and there's real money in that." She took another sip of her coffee. "I heard the first person to report the Happy Mountain fire was an independent spotter contracted to watch properties in Skylandia."

"What about the public firefighters—the Forest Service?

"Years ago, you'd hear that a bad apple set a fire so he'd get paid to fight it. But now fire is pretty much a given every year. They even stay on for prescribed burns in the off-season, if they're not totally worn out. So I don't hear those stories anymore."

"Anyone else?"

"Maybe people who don't like the changes happening in their towns or open spaces," Kelly said. "You know rural areas are growing in population fast since the pandemic, and that's annoying to some people. A few big fires that cause losses might discourage newcomers from moving in. And that's a good thing for the old-timers' open space and property values."

I shifted on the hard seat of my wobbly chair. The local homeowner she'd just described reminded me uncomfortably of my sweet, misanthropic Nathan. No more building in the forest. No more people, period. As if that was an option. I shook my head and asked, "Anyone else?"

"Well," she said, "there's me, I guess. What's insurance but a gamble on risk? Risk up, rates up. And insurance companies hire adjusters, analysts, salespeople, attorneys, expert witnesses—you know, people paid to undertake investigations and give their opinions about a dispute over an insurance claim or anything else that goes to trial."

"Do you know any expert fire witnesses from around here?"

"Sure," she said. "LaVonne Heath."

*****

It seemed like I hadn't been to the Three Bells in a decade—and maybe I hadn't. The old tavern stood just down the street from the Seattle Daily News building, where the roof still sported the rotating neon globe that had inspired Superman's creator. Not that anyone remembered Clark Kent's Daily Planet anymore.

And not that the Daily News staff worked from that gorgeous turn-of-the-20th-century building anymore. It had been sold off during one of Seattle's recent real estate booms and was destined for a future as high-end condominiums. Now, the newspaper's staff, such as it was, worked from home. Safer, was the feeling during the pandemic. Cheaper, was the reality now.

The Three Bells was the newspaper bar in Seattle. Every city used to have one. Walk in any time day or night and see whoever just got off deadline having themselves a little celebration. Tonight's gathering, though, was in memory of my friend Paula.

I wandered around the bar, warm pint of beer in my hand, wondering if I looked as old and disappointed as everyone else in the room. The former city editor, once a personage of seemingly unlimited power, sat alone at a scuffed four top nursing a mug of hot water garnished with lemon. The last person to hold the travel editor position—before it was eliminated in one of the endless rounds of budget cuts—stood at the bar, announcing to anyone who hesitated long enough that she hadn't taken a flight in two years. And the ex-chief of the editorial pages, a man who used to strike terror in anyone running for elected office, loitered by the appetizer table, gazing at the wan broccoli and beige ranch dip as if it could tell him where he'd gone wrong.

"Give us a fucking break already," said my friend Michael when I voiced my feelings about the crowd. "It's a sad occasion. Everybody loved Paula. Everybody misses Paula. Everybody is devastated by what happened to Paula. What do you expect us to be doing, a goddamn tap dance?"

I smiled in spite of myself and gazed across the barroom—and was startled when an older woman seated at a red leatherette booth smiled back at me. She wore a black knit dress that hugged her slender frame. A tasteful string of pearls encircled her long neck, and onyx earrings dangled from beneath her platinum bob. The effect, I thought, smoothing my gray T-shirt over my black go-to-town pants, was very sophisticated.

"Who's that?" I asked Michael.

"Oh, you mean Patricia Dylan?" he answered. "Used to be Pat Dylan, the investigative reporter?"

"No shit!" I said. "That's Pat Dylan?"

The woman waved, beckoning us to her booth.

"Patricia Dylan," Michael corrected.

"Beth!" the woman cried as we approached.

"Pat!" I said. "Patricia!"

We exchanged air kisses, and Michael and I sat on either side of a slit in the upholstery that was leaking stuffing fast. It didn't have much longer to live.

"So! What have you been doing with yourself?" I asked, immediately regretting my phrasing. "Looks like you've been busy."

"Oh, good God, Beth," Michael said. "I'll go get us another round. What are you having, Patricia?"

"Manhattan," she said. "No cherry."

She turned to me. "Well, I have been busy, as a matter of fact. Living in Madrona with my loving partner Hans. Two cats, Solange and Sidonie. I wrote a book about Amazon—the company, not the river, of course. And now I'm teaching at the writers' center." She smiled across the table at me. "I've never been happier."

I raised my warm beer and we clinked our nearly empty glasses.

"But what's this I hear about you?" she said. "Writing for a London tabloid?"

"Well," I said, "sort of. More like just a thing I do now and then."

"Bullshit. She's West Coast stringer for that scandal sheet The Informant." Michael carefully set our drinks on the table and slid in beside me. "She's working on a story right now about the wildfires, like the one that killed Paula. Evidence points toward arson, maybe."

"Arson," Patricia said carefully. "What makes you think that?"

"This will surprise you," I said, "but Michael is exaggerating." I picked up my new glass and took a long sip of the cold pilsner. "But it's the second series of fires that seem suspicious, the ones along the La Likt River. The couple accused of starting them say they saw somebody in the area just before the fires were reported. His behavior seemed odd." I glanced down at my hands, embarrassed. "I really don't have a lot more than that—just a man at the scene of the fires, maybe throwing his fast food trash out the window of his Camaro."

"That's not nothing," said Patricia. She took a sip of her drink and placed it on the smudged table. "This is before your time, but I covered the Phantom arsonist back in the early '90s. I don't suppose you remember him?"

Michael and I shook our heads.

"Well," Patricia said, pushing back her blonde hair with fingernails painted fire engine red, "he's the most prolific arsonist in state history. He set at least 96 fires—some think a lot more—and all in a six-month period. Most resulted only in property damage, but he did kill three residents of a retirement home when he set a bed on fire."

I gasped and Michael said, "Holy crap! That's messed up."

Patricia took another quick sip and nodded. "He definitely was messed up. I interviewed him before his sentencing. His attorney thought a sympathetic story might influence the judge."

She smiled into her drink and gave it a quick swirl. "The Phantom told me he liked to set multiple fires at the same time. He enjoyed watching the firefighters scramble to contain everything all at once."

She shook her head. "Anyway, the interview didn't work out the way his attorney planned. The Phantom arsonist is in state prison now. He's only got," she paused, ticking off the fingernails of her right hand with the fleshy part of her thumb, "let's see . . . 67 years left on his sentence."

"Wow," I said. "What a story!"

"Yes," Patricia said. "But the point is, he wasn't a criminal mastermind. He was just a guy driving around looking for the opportunity to set something on fire—no fancy tools, no special accelerants, just the occasional can of gas and a Bic lighter. Sort of like your man—just a guy tossing something out of his car into dry grass during the longest drought in state history."

"So, how did they catch him?" I asked. "Did the cops have a sketch or a behavioral profile or—"

I was interrupted by the blare of the television above the bar. I turned to see the former city editor wielding the remote, just as he had back in the newsroom.

"New at six o'clock," the anchor announced. "Fire has broken out for the second time this week in rural Sahaptin County and is now threatening multimillion-dollar homes in the Skylandia resort. Law enforcement officials have released a sketch of this man, calling him a person of interest seen near the point of ignition."

A police image of a middle-aged white man, prominent nose, floppy salt-and-pepper hair with a matching beard, appeared on the screen. He wore a red baseball hat.

"Hey Beth," Michael said, "Doesn't that look a lot like your husband?"

Part 3: The Rocky Ridge Fire

Chapter 10

Nathan tours the hoosegow

I always thought I might enjoy a little time in jail.

Eliminate distractions. No chores or decisions. Time to read and write. Some long-neglected upper body work. If the food was decent and your partners in crime similarly inclined, why not? A few months locked away might take the place of a yoga retreat or a stay at one of those pricey Santa Barbara monasteries.

The look on Bill Chaney's face counseled against this view.

Yesterday, Bill followed me all the way down I-90 to the Sahaptin County Public Safety Building—aka the county jail—in Ellensburg. My ride was in the back of the sheriff's patrol car. Bill had seen the cop cars parked in front of our cabin and had run down the street from his place just in time to spot me being hauled from the garage and arrested by Sheriff Peters and his lieutenant. By the time I was booked into a cell in the county's windowless concrete structure—right across the street from E-Burg Brewing where I more typically spent my time—Bill was right there acting as my attorney.

This morning, he was back to check on me and gather details. He also delivered a few personal items I'd requested, including pencils, paper, and a hard copy of the new 500-page report from the Intergovernmental Panel on Climate Change. We sat in a small room across a rectangular metal table from each other, just like you see in the movies. The door even had a tiny window that the sergeant could peek through.

"So, it's mostly circumstantial stuff," said Bill, arms crossed on the table, his freshly shaved face looming in front of me. "We'll get to that. But it's really about your blog. About the woodpecker habitat? And the new one, about how Skylandia never should've been built?"

"Yeah. I was just trying to add a different perspective, a longer-term view."

"Right," Bill said. "But some people see clear motives for arson there."

I stared at him.

"If they didn't know you, I mean."

I shrugged. "I can't say what I think?"

"I quote," Bill began, slipping on his Foster Grant cheaters to read from his notes, "'Nothing like a good old-fashioned catastrophe to change some minds.'"

"But I'm pretty sure I didn't actually say that in the blog," I protested, momentarily confused.

Bill straightened, removed his glasses, and grimaced.

"An attorney should never ask this," he said. "But I'm your friend, Nathan. Did you do it?"

"Of course not," I said. "I would never set a fire. Even in a place that's doomed to burn."

"Had nothing to do with it? Not working with a friend? Maybe one of your High Country Crapper colleagues?"

"Bill, give me a break."

"Had to put it out there," he mumbled, sounding only partially relieved and aiming his hangdog face down toward his notes.

"But," I inserted into his glum silence, using the single syllable as a placeholder to give myself time to formulate my next thought.

"You asked about friends." I cleared my throat as the image of Twyla running through the forest in her shorts again played in my mind.

"What?" Bill reluctantly asked.

"Some things that Twyla said—you know Twyla, the new bartender at Dave's?—made me wonder if she, well, if she or somebody she knew might be capable of setting a fire."

"Really? What'd she say?"

"It's likely nothing," I said, now fully stuck on the mental video loop of Twyla crouching, then prancing away from a flaming bundle of matches on the forest floor. "I actually like her. But when we were birdwatching she kept asking me about 'direct action' and what would change minds about building in the forests."

"Interesting," Bill said flatly. "You were birdwatching with her. When she said this."

For an attorney, my friend didn't have much of a poker face. This particular far-away look told me at least part of Bill's brain was now weighing the possibility that I was turning on Twyla—my new lover and associate in arson—and setting her up to take the fall. Bill and Kathy held season tickets along with Beth and me to the Seattle Film Noir Festival and repeated exposure to bitter endings in the dark shadows of life made us suggestive when it came to the bleak reality of human nature.

"Just an observation," I concluded with a hand flick. "I'm sure she's fine."

How had it come to this, I wondered. Me in the hot seat ratting out my duplicitous femme fatale. Just last week Bill, Dave, and I were merrily polishing off a growler of beer on the Chaney's immaculate backyard patio as we grilled chicken breasts not more than an arm's length from Mr. Clucker's home.

"It's just a couple of things she said," I said, trying again to snap Bill out of his reverie. "Probably nothing."

"Her son fits the arson demo better," Bill said, still looking lost in the alleyways of duped Joes and desperate blondes.

"Glenn seems really bright," I said. "But I suppose, if he was trying to please his mother? It's possible." I felt creepy about throwing suspicion off myself by implicating a high school student. But I had just moved my mouth to do exactly that.

"Something to check out," Bill said, tapping the table with all his fingertips. "Definitely."

With that unconvincing remark, we both seemed to shuffle back into the bright lobby of reality.

"Now, let's get to it," he continued. "They think you were up in the Skylandia development yesterday," he continued, "right before the fire started."

"Well, I was up there," I said. "I was riding my mountain bike around the Old Sawmill neighborhood, looking for Penny. I thought she'd run away again."

"Beth tells me Penny was with Nigel," Bill said. "You didn't know?"

"I didn't think they'd be gone that long. Nigel's not a dog person."

"Yeah, who figured?" said Bill. "Breaking News: Nigel and Penny Save the Little Girl, right?"

"Let's give Holly some credit, too."

"Anyway. The investigators found a bike bell near the suspected ignition site. Do you have a bell on your bike?"

"It was a little round bell painted like a baseball," I said.

"Was?"

"Must've fallen off sometime. Not sure when."

"Well, they found it in some trees off the fourteenth tee on the Coal River Golf Course."

Bill and I had played that course a dozen times. He was a three handicapper and I was a duffer, but he liked having me along, perhaps in the same way that some high-strung race horses enjoy the company of a small goat.

"One-of-a-kind bell," he noted for the record.

Then it hit me. "Wait, I was nowhere near the Coal River course yesterday," I said, leaning forward. "I only cruised the Old Sawmill area, clear on the other side of the development, closer to Patrick."

"Any idea how the bell got to the golf course?"

"Maybe it was stolen? Maybe fell off on a previous ride?" I suggested. "Beth and I ride up there all the time. Got the place to ourselves during the midweek. I'm not really sure when the bell went missing. Could've been weeks ago. Months."

"Gotcha," he said, deflated by my answer. He took a minute to shuffle his files, glancing up at me a couple times. I couldn't believe this. Was he waiting for me to reconsider? To confess?

"Now, the sketch of the suspect," he resumed, sounding even more downhearted.

From his file he extracted the computer-generated image of the person of interest. I studied the face as Bill filled me in, his voice gruff. "Lady from Skylandia was playing an early round with a friend. After the fire broke out, she reported seeing this guy in the woods near the fourteenth hole. Got a close look. Said he was lanky and "furtive." Bill made quotation marks in the air with his pointer and middle fingers. "Lime green shirt. She worked with investigators to come up with the picture."

"And this is what they ran on the news yesterday?" I asked.

"Yep."

"And why I was arrested?"

"Seems so. Somebody called in and said it looked like you. Anonymous tip."

"Well," I said, "I guess it does look a bit like me."

"Kind of a generic unshaven white guy, I'd say."

"That's me, so I've been told." I studied the picture. "But the hat
—" The guy in the sketch wore a bright red baseball cap with a
QAnon logo on the front. "I don't have one of those," I said.
"Obviously."

"No, I didn't think so," Bill said. "That's good. Should help."

"Actually, though," I said slowly, "the shirt looks like one of
mine." Bill pursed his lips and furrowed his bushy eyebrows. He
held the expression. Apparently unable to unhear my last statement,
he looked down at the picture and mumbled, "Lots of green fleece
shirts out there."

"Sherpa brand. Lime green with an orange pocket," I said,
pointing to the image. "Never seen another like it."

Bill's lowered head now rested in his big mitts.

*****

Bill Chaney spent most of the rest of the day working with Beth
on coming up with bail. If the district attorney decided to push for a
Class A arson charge, the sentence could be life in prison. Bill
thought that unlikely, but depending on the exact charge he said we
would probably need hundreds of thousands of dollars to post bond.
Which meant using our townhouse on Queen Anne Hill as collateral.

Meanwhile, Bill was contacting attorneys who could represent me
in criminal court and following up on leads that might make the DA
hesitate to press charges. In particular, he hired a private investigator
to find out if anyone at Rocky Ridge had seen me riding my bike
near the Old Sawmill. Character references were also being rounded
up, as Bill said, "to counterbalance those fire-related blogs of yours."
I had no idea if he was pursuing my lead about Twyla. I felt bad for
even mentioning her.

As I waited for Beth's visit in the afternoon, I stretched out on the
cot for a good session with the thick climate report Bill had

delivered. Talk about context! All the tribulations of one man in central Washington state are trivial compared to the tenuous fate of half the earth's species due to climate change. Heat events, flooding, wildfires, migration, political chaos—it's all coming our way. I was grateful for the solid four hours of reading, however grim.

My lunch—a bologna sandwich and a small bag of Fritos—hit the spot, as did the 20-minute nap afterward.

When Beth arrived, she found me refreshed—sipping a large coffee from a Styrofoam cup and jotting notes for my next blog.

"Nathan," she said, tugging the pages out of my lap. "Stop with the blogs already. Look where it got you. Good thing you can't have your laptop in here."

"But it's my newsletter, Beth," I said. "My subscribers are all on board. They're all Drake Water Quality Project supporters. I've never had complaints."

"Crimany! You're worse than your father, Nathan." She was literally pulling her hair straight out from the sides of her head. The strands didn't come out in her hands, but it looked painful. "Don't you know that anybody can Google you and find your website and your newsletter?"

"Well, theoretically, yes," I said. "But—"

"Of course they do! That's why they're calling you a peckerwood! It's why they ransacked our house! It's why you're an arson suspect! In jail!" Beth punctuated this last point with two quick jabs to my chest with right pointer, then sighed as if her admirable store of fighting spirit had finally been depleted. "Great Caesar's Ghost," she added mournfully, dropping her head and then squeezing it, that poor sweet melon caught in the vise of her raised forearms. Again, it looked painful. I reached out and gently lowered her arms to her side and wrapped my arms around her. We weren't supposed to touch, but the officer on duty—a Seahawks fan, of course—had been kinder to me since I'd thoroughly dissed the San Francisco 49ers.

"I suppose my next few blogs could focus on climate change," I said. "How could I be blamed for that?"

I felt her tense under my grip. She groaned in exasperation but said nothing.

"I'm sorry," I said. "Twyla told me I should tone it down too."

Beth pushed me away. "Well, don't mind me. If your new girlfriend is telling you to cease and desist, you better listen to her. What does the beautiful Twyla say? Twyla the birdwatcher. Twyla the beer girl."

"I went birdwatching with her once," I said.

"That was a nice long day you had together."

"You've been busy with Nigel," I countered. "You've been wrapped up with Paula's affairs."

"I work with Nigel," she said heatedly. "And, oh that's right, now it's Twyla the journalist too, isn't it? You've already got a journalist at home, Nathan. Why do you need another?"

Again, I moved toward her and slowly wrapped my arms around her. "I'm sorry, Beth," I said. "I just thought you wanted to be on your own for a while." A pause, then: "Are you doing okay sorting out all of Paula's stuff? That's a lot on your plate. Can I help somehow?"

"You're in jail, Honey," she pointed out, slumping in my arms, her head pressing into the saddle of my neck and shoulder.

"Maybe you can bust me out."

"I'm doing okay, considering," she said eventually, her face now moist on my shoulder. "The gathering at Three Bells was hard. Lots of memories. God, finding her in the truck. Of all people."

I just held her.

"And now, there's Brooklyn's situation."

Beth had spoken to Bill about Paula's estate plan and custody arrangements. What had seemed like a long shot when Beth signed the papers making her Brooklyn's guardian in the event of a disaster now seemed entirely likely.

"We'll do whatever we need to, Beth," I said.

"James is trying," she said. "But he may not be ready."

"We'll take Brooklyn," I found myself saying.

Once the words were out, the decision apparently made, I was surprised to look around and find what had changed: absolutely nothing. We were still a childless couple. We were still in a tiny cell in the Sahaptin County Public Safety Building. Nothing had changed, but the light in the cell was definitely different. Beth's hair. My books. Everything sharper, almost vibrating. Nothing had changed, but my vision was suddenly acute and my thinking on every topic—the future, our relationship, the purpose of life—was boldly precise as if the tips on all my neuronal axons had miraculously been scrubbed and polished after decades of neglect.

She squeezed me and the dampness on my shoulder spread.

After a long period of quiet, Beth and I sat on my cot, held hands, and talked about the mundane task of posting bail. Where the money would come from. How much it would cost.

"Also," she said, getting up to go, "I did what Bill asked and made a list of what went missing from our house after the break-in. You're right, I couldn't find your lime fleece shirt. I couldn't find your green Gore-Tex jacket either, but maybe it's in Seattle. Your Italian hiking boots also seem to be missing."

"Those could be out in the garage," I said. "I was waterproofing them before the chimps arrived."

"And your baseball hats, the Mariners cap and—you remember—the red Queen Anne hat. They aren't on the hook by the door. They left your Birdfest hat."

"Okay," I said. "Thanks for doing that."

"Hey, before I leave," said Beth. "I wasn't going to say anything, but on my way through the parking lot I met a few of those guys who were hanging out with Roger Thorp at the community meeting."

"You recognized them?" I asked.

"They seemed to recognize me."

"How did—"

"Nigel and I did an interview with them. Kind of. Anyway, these guys outside were setting up for a demonstration. Against you. Had a couple signs. 'Woodpeckers or Humans?' 'Drake is an Enviro-arsonist.' That's all I saw."

"What did they say to you?"

"They got kind of close and told me arsonists should be hung."

"Hey, Lou," I immediately yelled toward the door. I got up and pounded on it a couple of times. "Lou," I yelled out of the little window, "you got some crazies in the parking lot harassing my wife."

"We're aware of their presence," came the voice from outside the door.

"You need to give her some protection before she goes back out there."

There was a pause before the reply.

"Yeah, we'll take care of it."

"Nathan," Beth said slowly, "this will sound weird, probably, but maybe it's a good thing you're in jail."

"What?"

"I mean, because there are people outside who—" She paused. "Well, who might mean you harm. I'll ask Bill what he thinks."

My stay in the Sahaptin County Correctional Facility might be longer than I expected.

"Beth," I asked as the sergeant escorted her out, "Next time you come maybe you can bring me a package of fig newtons. And volume five of Knausgaard."

Chapter 11

Beth considers the descent of man

"What the authorities didn't realize," my editor was telling the admiring crowd gathered around him, "is that to find a monkey, one must think like a monkey." He tapped his temple with one long finger, then reached for his pint of beer.

I stifled the urge to point out that a chimp is not a monkey, which is just one of the essential facts Nigel got wrong in the story of his triumphant rescue mission, presently trending on The Informant's website. Now we sat at the round corner table in Dave's brew pub— my favorite perch—while Nigel's adoring public bought him beer after beer. Penny, valiant search and rescue dog, was curled up in her old spot behind the bar. Under Nigel's guidance, she seemed to have regained her earlier angelic nature.

As Nigel reached the apex of his story—"the chimp and I achieved a mind-meld, and she gently handed the child to me"—I loudly snorted. Nigel leaned in close to me. "I have street cred now," he hissed in my ear. "It is an advantage, Mary Beth. Do not ruin this."

I extracted myself from Nigel's circle—Jamie the hairstylist quickly took my place—and sat at the bar, where Dave gave me a sympathetic half-smile and a schooner of root beer.

"But Brooklyn's okay," he reminded me.

Tears seeped into my eyes and I tried to push the image of Paula's body behind the wheel of her truck aside. Of course, I was ecstatic about Brooklyn. She was my friend's granddaughter and the source of the one bit of good news in our town since the fires began. Her recovery was cause for joy. No doubt.

No doubt.

When I signed the papers, becoming Brooklyn's guardian had seemed like a remote chance. Now the thought that I might soon be responsible for a two-year-old churned and tumbled in my mind along with every other unknowable outcome in my suddenly out-of-control life.

I told myself to take things one step at a time, and step one was to make sure Brooklyn was safe. But I couldn't keep other questions from pushing their way to the front of my mind, where the angry mob of memories lifted their war banners and charged forward. Were Nathan and I ready to take on her guardianship? Enroll her in kindergarten, attend her soccer games, teach her to drive? Did we need to move to a bigger town with a better school district? Start a college fund? How would I explain our sudden parenthood to the other preschool mothers? How, for the love of Mike, would I explain it to Brooklyn?

I closed my eyes and rotated my bar stool toward the door. Breathe in through your nose, I told myself. Breathe out through your mouth. Now open your eyes.

Jamie the hairdresser placed her hand consolingly on Nigel's left forearm as he recounted the deep rush of emotion, the, ehm, pure joy he had experienced upon seeing Brooklyn on the monkey's lap. It was spiritual, he told his admirers. That's what it was.

I left off my breathing exercises and scowled. As childish as it was, I couldn't help feeling jealous that Nigel got the role of the hero. While I was attending my friend's wake, Nigel and Penny had entered a burned-out townhome complex and executed the heroic rescue of a darling toddler—who was being cared for by a chimpanzee, no less. Stories like that don't come around in every career. And where was I when this one magically presented itself to

Nigel, thanks to the skills of my very own dog? In a coffee shop, talking about fire insurance.

It was galling.

But yes. Of course I was happy about Brooklyn. Of course I was. The little girl was dehydrated and sunburned, but otherwise in good shape. Nathan and I wanted to take her in immediately. What was one more person, and a small one at that, in the overstuffed cabin? But she'd quickly been placed under the care of Child Protective Services until they could sort out our "complex living arrangement." Or so they said.

"Might have been better for her to stay with Holly," Cassie muttered when she heard the news.

Cassie, of course, was still camped out in our second bedroom, tending to her superhumanly strong chimps in our half-built garage. James was battling addiction on the sagging couch in our living room. Nigel, preferring our kitchen table to his perfectly good Formica desk at the Sno-Cap Motel, was perennially underfoot. And Big Red had joined Penny in the perpetually under repair dog run.

Look at it from the state's point of view: was it a good environment for a two-year-old?

At least I'd had a room to myself recently since my husband was in the county jail on a felony arson charge. I'd spent the last 18 hours filling out the paperwork that put our townhome in Seattle on the line to raise his bail money. Bill Chaney, attorney at law, was down in Ellensburg right now, trying to spring Nathan from the pokey.

"You should probably stay away," Bill said when I showed up at his door, ready to march up to the warden and free my man. "I'm told the protesters are still in the parking lot. You'll just inflame them, and that's not good for Nathan."

And so here I was, listening to Nigel hold forth on search and rescue techniques and chimp psychology. At least I'd been able to use the time to set up an appointment with the owner of the Bullfrog

Quick Stop, the gas station the Lundquists said they'd visited on the evening the La Likt River fires started. The station's owner Samar and I were going to go over the security camera video together. I glanced at the time on my phone, then pushed off from Dave's polished bar.

"Beth! Where are you off to?" Nigel pointed his sharp, red nose my way.

"Just over to check out the gas station video," I answered. "Boring, factual stuff of no interest to you."

"Yes, well, I'll come along anyway," he said, staggering to his feet. "For support, you know. It's been a hard couple of days for the Drakes, hasn't it? Not a lot of success."

"A chimp," I hissed at him, "is not a monkey."

*****

Samar's Bullfrog Quick Stop is well known along the I-90 corridor between Spokane and Seattle. It's got 24 functioning gas pumps, a convenience store containing a fried chicken franchise, and air-conditioned restrooms that are the cleanest this side of Singapore.

Samar met us at the convenience store counter just as Nigel was picking up an order of chicken nuggets. "Let's use my office," he said. "I have us all set up." He motioned to a white door secured with three prominent deadbolts that stood just beyond the chicken franchise's bank of fill-it-yourself soda spigots.

The Bullfrog Quick Stop offered the full line of Pepsi products. You got a free refill if you bought their 32-ounce, high quality plastic MegaMug, plus a dollar off every time you returned to reuse it. This, I'm sad to say, is how I developed my Diet Pepsi problem. It had been tough to kick, and I kept my eyes straight ahead as we passed the tempting row of soda nozzles. Just hearing the satisfying click the machines made as you jammed your quart-size cup up against the "on" switch was enough to trigger my craving.

"A moment!" said Nigel. "Getting my drink." Bewildered, he jabbed at the ice machine's wire handle until a cascade of cubes overwhelmed his MegaMug and tumbled to the floor. Nigel was delighted. "I simply love your generosity with ice," he said. "It's one of the true markers of a fully realized society."

Samar's office was small and crowded with road trip-related supplies. Stacks of blue paper towels for replenishing the windshield-washing stations sat on silver wire shelving alongside plastic jugs of cooking oil for the chicken. Shrink-wrapped packs of Five Hour Energy Drink shared a corner with a tower of plastic crates holding colorful bags of pork rinds. Befitting their status, cigarettes and alcohol were set off in their own special locked cage.

Samar placed three chairs around his neat, metal desk—two folding chairs with plastic seats on either side of a desk chair with rollers and a wood-beaded New York taxi seat cover. A monitor and a keyboard covered in thick plastic sat in the middle of the desk. Nigel placed his chicken nuggets and MegaMug next to it, then planted himself in the desk chair.

I made sure I banged into Nigel hard when Samar and I scooted our folding chairs as close as possible to the monitor. "If you don't mind," Samar said, stretching to place his fingers on the keyboard.

A black and white image of the Quick Stop's gas plaza popped up on the screen. "I pulled the footage from last Thursday, early evening," Samar said. "It's not a very busy time for us, so if that couple with the van stopped by, we'll probably spot them."

On the screen, the station was empty but for a sedan that had taken a hit to the rear passenger door serious enough to require securing with a length of rope. The driver pulled decisively into the drive-through lane at Sami's Quick Stop Coffee—did I mention the station also serves some of the best espresso in town?—and there she idled, arm flapping out of the window as if to hurry the process along.

Meanwhile, the action at the pumps was all around Number Seven, where a woman driving a Subaru Outback was filling her tank. A half-ton pickup pulled in, creeping uncomfortably close to the Subaru driver, who looked up nervously.

Samar made a move to fast-forward through the footage, but Nigel grabbed his hand. "A moment!" he said. "The station's empty. Why doesn't the truck driver simply move to another pump?"

"Ah, well, that's Jerri Schmidt," Samar said. "You know, from Jerri's Smoke 'n' Spit in town?" When our faces remained blank, he added, "She always uses Number Seven. Thinks it's lucky."

Samar tapped a key and the footage leapt forward in jerky flashes. "Hold up!" I said as another vehicle—a battered Toyota truck—moved from its spot by the pumps to a space in front of the convenience store.

"That's Dave, isn't it?" Nigel asked. "From the brewery?"

"Sure does look like his truck," I said as we watched the man enter the store. "Is he just picking up his change or what?"

The three of us stared at the screen for several long minutes. Finally, Dave reappeared.

"Crimany!" I said. "What took so long?"

"Sometimes," Samar said hesitantly, "well, sometimes a customer will stop in to use the restroom."

"Dave lives here, though," I said. "Like five minutes away. Wouldn't think he'd need your restroom."

"Still, Mary Beth, they are very nice restrooms," Nigel said. "Air-conditioned. Good quality tissues. And spotless." He turned to our host. "Really, excellent job on the cleaning." Samar acknowledged the praise with a slight nod while Nigel continued explaining Dave's behavior to me. "Sometimes, especially when one's own home is, ehm, fully occupied," he said, "or the loo perhaps a bit sluggish for one's projected needs, it's a real pleasure to treat oneself to a pleasant experience elsewhere."

As Dave's truck left the gas plaza, another vehicle—an open-topped Jeep this time—pulled in. The driver parked near the entry to the convenience store in a space reserved for people with disabilities. He jauntily hopped out of the Jeep and headed inside. I could just make out a head topped by curly hair in his passenger seat—somebody waiting.

"Isn't that Tommy DeRoux's Jeep?" I asked Samar. Tommy and his brother Cody sometimes did odd jobs for us at the cabin. They came from a family with a long history in the county, not all of it savory. In fact, it was the DeRoux brothers who bred Penny and her brother Big Red, back when they thought Vizslas would make them rich. Nathan managed to convince them to get out of the dog breeding business, and I have to admit that over time I've come to feel somewhat protective of them. I squinted at the screen. "Who's that with him?"

Samar looked uncomfortable. "I'm not sure we should be looking at this. Privacy rights and all."

"Nonsense," said Nigel as Tommy exited the Quick Stop's store. He paused and shook a small, brown paper bag triumphantly in the direction of his passenger.

Nigel sat back in the desk chair and swiveled toward Samar. "Well, he certainly looks pleased. What's he got in that bag?"

"Personal items," Samar said unhappily. "Just some cigarettes and," he paused, "items of a personal nature. For health."

Nigel and I looked at each other. "For health, huh," I said. "Can't be the fried chicken then."

"Oh, my lord." Nigel clapped his hands gleefully. "Condoms! Tommy DeRoux has a sweetheart."

"Get out!" I blurted, giving Nigel a little jab in his bony arm. "Who is it?" We bumped heads painfully as we both tried to get a better look at the screen. "Looks kind of like my yoga teacher at the studio up in Patrick, but she's married. Does this thing have a zoom function, Samar?"

But Samar was already advancing the video. "Not what you're looking for," he said. "Moving on."

The images flashed and jerked while Samar steadfastly ignored our pleading to pause the video whenever we spotted a vehicle we recognized. Finally, a Mercedes Sprinter van pulled in and lingered by the air and water station long enough for us to make a positive ID.

"There they are!" I yelped as Samar took his finger off fast-forward.

The light was fading from the day when the van arrived at the Bullfrog Quick Stop. On the screen, the gas station plaza was an island of white light surrounded by a dark landscape broken only by the twin high beams of passing cars as they tried to pierce the smoky air. Two light gray figures emerged from the van.

"I think that's Walt getting out from the driver's side," I said. "And Eleanor from the passenger side."

"Wait," Samar said. "We have another camera on that side of the building. Let me switch and we'll see if we can make out the plates." He tapped the keyboard and the scene changed to the northwest side of the property, with the air and water station front and center.

"BRDWCHR," I read from the Sprinter's front plate. "That's them."

On the screen, Walt placed his fingers on the small of his back and gave it a stretch. Eleanor walked stiffly toward the convenience store. She was bound for the restroom, if the story they'd told me was true. The figure on the screen stopped abruptly and looked to her left. Walt was pointing in the same direction. Soon, both were gazing at something just at the edge of our picture.

"Can we switch to another view and see what they're looking at?" I asked Samar.

He shook his head. "But it looks like a car," he said, pausing the image. "A sedan?"

"We're seeing a low bumper there?" Nigel asked. "Perhaps the front fender?"

"Some kind of sports car?" I added.

Samar started the video again and we watched Walt inspect the van, making a slow circumnavigation. If there was a tow chain attached, we couldn't see it. Evidently satisfied, Walt started toward the restroom.

"Better safe than sorry," Nigel muttered.

As Walt disappeared into the convenience store, a figure came into view on the screen. A man was striding confidently toward the Sprinter van.

"Beth," said Nigel. "What's your husband doing there?"

Looking neither left nor right, Nathan walked directly to the rear of the van. In one swift movement, he crouched down, bent at the waist, and seemed to make a repair underneath the van. A second or two passed, then he straightened and walked quickly to the left, out of our frame. In the next moment Walt and Eleanor emerged from the store holding hands, newly washed, presumably. Reaching the van, they parted, took their seats, and exited the gas station. Pinpricks of light marked their passage—sparks off a hanging tow chain.

I was dumbfounded. "It can't be Nathan," I whispered.

"Can it really not be Nathan?" Nigel asked. "After all, the man is in jail on an arson charge. That seems to line up quite well."

I glared at Nigel, then asked if we could see the video again.

Nathan, or nearly Nathan, bent to the back bumper of the van. "Freeze it there, please," I said. "Zoom in, Samar, if you can."

"Is that grease on the back of his hand?" Nigel asked, his nose nearly touching the monitor.

"Looks like a tat," Samar said. He zoomed in again, but the screen went blurry, so he eased the view out. "Maybe 'LA' on the right hand. For Los Angeles?"

"And on the left," Nigel squinted, then fell back in his chair. "Too blurred to say for sure, but I think it could be 'SF.'"

"Can't imagine somebody who loves the Dodgers and the Giants," I said.

"Or maybe it's '5-P?'" said Nigel, again nosing toward the screen.

"I can't tell what it is," I said. "And Nathan doesn't have any tattoos."

The three of us watched as Samar made the figure on the screen go backward, then forward, then backward again and forward again four more times. Each time, the man bent to the van's undercarriage, paused there as if fixing something, then straightened and walked quickly to his left.

It was the confident walking that finally convinced me. "It looks like Nathan," I said, "But Nathan doesn't walk like that. With Nathan, it's more like a loping gait—an up-and-down, side-to-side movement along with the forward motion. Not efficient, like this guy. With Nathan, it's, it's—"

"Ungainly?" Nigel supplied.

I chose to ignore him. "You know those illustrations of the evolution of man, where man starts out as an ape on all fours and in each iteration, he loses hair and gains height until finally we get to modern day?"

Nigel and Samar nodded.

"Nathan walks kind of like the second guy from the front of the line."

We all thought about that for a minute, then Samar asked, "if it's not Nathan, then who is it?"

Nigel quickly swiveled toward me just as I turned to look at him. The answer had come to us almost simultaneously.

Chapter 12

Our guest today, Nathan Drake

TRANSCRIPT OF "THE STRAIGHT TALK" PROGRAM
[Music playing: SOULFUL COUNTRY ACOUSTIC GUITAR]

Matty the Producer: *[Music playing]* It's the Voice of Colockum Ridge: Roooo-ger Thorp!

Thorp: Hello and welcome back, Sahaptin County—and points beyond. Matty and I are coming to you again from our studio high above the little city of Kittitas and the big burg itself, Ellensburg. Bringing you The Straight Talk you just can't get anywhere else.

[Music playing: LOUD GUITAR LICKS]

Matty: Coming to you thanks to Roger's sponsors and friends: Mid-County Plow, McCoy American Firearms and Home Safety, Sahaptin Hay Exporters, the Oba Corporation, MyFamilyFirst.com, and WorkCoin: the only crypto that values your work. And now Roooo-ger Thorp!

Thorp: Thank you, Matty. Our guest today, Nathan Drake. Nathan, why, thank you for taking the time to visit us up here at Colockum Ridge Studios.

Drake: I wanted to speak directly to your listeners.

Thorp: Nice surprise. And you brought with you?

Drake: This is my attorney, Bill Chaney.

Thorp: We'll just be chatting today. Friendly back and forth. Welcome, Bill and Nathan.

Drake: Thank you, Roger.

Thorp: Now, for those of you just catching up, Nathan is from Seattle. Runs a nonprofit called High Country Crapper.

Drake: The Drake Water Quality Project. The goal is to provide clean toilets in the backcountry. One of the—

Thorp: I've always wondered about those things. Now Nathan, isn't one of the simple pleasures of the backcountry just taking care of your own business in the woods?

Drake: Well, Roger, in most places, that's still the way to go.

Thorp: There you go. No need for a socialized sanitation facility, right?

Drake: Not everywhere, no.

Thorp: Another case of government overreach.

Drake: But here's the thing. So many natural areas today—the Pacific Crest Trail, the North Cascades, even the Teanaway in our own backyard here—they attract too many people to allow the business-as-usual approach.

Thorp: You're telling me I need to pee into one of those things every time I need to take a leak?

Drake: Good question. When you're—

Thorp: Like if I get up out of my tent in the middle of the night?

Drake: Well, of course the proximity of salt-loving ungulates is always a factor in—

Thorp: Nathan, maybe we should move on to what brings you here today.

Drake: Sure, the fires. There are a couple of points—

Thorp: You were arrested for arson in the Rocky Ridge fire. Just got out on bail, correct?

Drake: Technically yes, I was in jail. But at the arraignment I pleaded not guilty. The fire teams really just wanted to ask me about a few blogs I wrote that could be misinterpreted—

Thorp: Misinterpreted. Let's see. You said here, I quote: "Fire is a dynamic part of the forest ecology. And biogeography."

Drake: Fire is an integral part of our east-slope Ponderosa-Douglas fir Cascades bioregion. We need—

Thorp: Those of us who work the land know all about fire. It's simple, actually. We don't need more government reports. We've been managing this land for three-four generations. As hunters, our taxes on guns and ammo pay for wildlife restoration. We love this land.

Drake: Ranchers and loggers and hunters certainly do play an important role in managing our western lands.

Thorp: Glad we agree. The problem as I see it was all those folks who studied ecology in college and then came out here and told us not to cut anything. Protecting the spotted owls and salamanders. That's why our forests are overgrown and burning up today, right?

Drake: It's actually a myth that—

Thorp: Now, Drake, you also said, and I quote, "Skylandia is like kindling and wind-whipped fire is certain to visit them someday." Sounds kind of like a Bible prophecy to me.

Drake: Just facts. Skylandia sits right in the middle of—

Thorp: You a religious man, Nathan?

Drake: I don't see—

Thorp: Because that sounds kind of biblical. Here's another. You said, "Nothing like a good old-fashioned catastrophe to hit the reset."

Drake: I never wrote that on the blog. I'd be curious to know where you—

Thorp: I got it right here. Anyway, I could see how some people might interpret these words of yours to mean that you set the Rocky Ridge fire.

Drake: I did not set any fires. I do believe fire is a natural part of our lands. We need to adapt to it with sensible building codes, firesafe best practices, proper financial incentives, and—

Thorp: Well, I suppose our fellow citizens, our jury members, here in Sahaptin County will decide if you're guilty. Now—what's that? Oh my. I believe your lawyer wants a word with you, Nathan. He's waving like mad. Yeah. Go ahead, we'll take a little break while you confab with your attorney.

[Music playing: LOUD GUITAR LICKS]

Thorp: Hey friends, your family deserves more. You've been working your butt off, but the system is rigged against you. The IRS sniper teams. The big banks and investment companies. Those woke guys in the cities who don't actually produce anything. They've been getting rich, buying up the big ranches, changing our towns to be more like the cities they just left. Well. I'm here to tell you how you can finally get what you deserve. It's WorkCoin. A brand new cryptocurrency that is taking off like a rocket ship. Now, regular listeners know I bought in just a year ago, and as of today my shares are up something like ten times over. Matty, what're you, up about double in just a couple weeks? Yeah. And I'll tell you this: We are not fooling you, folks. Nor are we selling our coins. No way. This thing is solid as Mount Stuart and it's just starting. Join me. I want y'all to be part of this.

Now, listen up. WorkCoin is being offered only on select radio broadcasts around the U.S. WorkCoin is completely separate from any Federal Reserve or World Bank influence. So, WorkCoin is the safe investment for those of us who value our freedoms. You own it and no banker in New York or Singapore can monkey it away from you. When the peanut butter hits the fan—and you know it will—WorkCoin will be there, in your survival shelter with your other supplies, working for you.

WorkCoin values work, and works for those with values. Go to our website and get on board.

[Music playing: SEARING GUITAR]

Thorp: All righty, Nathan Drake, accused arsonist, are you all lawyered up? Ready to talk some more?

Drake: Roger, if I may, I'd like to read a statement.

150

Thorp: Got a manifesto there, do you?

Drake: It's brief.

Thorp: Better than the Unabomber. Go for it.

Drake: I just wanted to make sure that your listeners know a few things about me before they convict me of something I didn't do.

Thorp: You do look a bit like Kaczynski, actually. All ears, Nate.

Drake: Number one: I had nothing to do with the Rocky Ridge fire. I was looking for my dog up in that area the day the fire started, but I was nowhere near the fire's actual ignition point.

Thorp: But didn't a lady golfer see you there?

Drake: Number two—

Thorp: And didn't the sheriff get up a sketch that looks exactly like you and, in fact, thanks to a good citizen, led to your arrest?

Drake: Number two: My home has been vandalized and my wife has been threatened by some who think, wrongly, that I set the fire. This is unacceptable. Let all the facts come out and let the law work. Anybody who confronts my wife and—

Thorp: Couldn't agree more. Folks, his wife's the one always reporting on us for the big media companies in England. Sure does make us look colorful. Some might say like hicks.

Drake: Okay, then. Number three: If anyone has problems with my blog posts, feel free to write to me or even call me to discuss it. Matters of science can be debated. There are unknowns. There is room for civilized discourse.

Thorp: This program is founded on civilized discourse.

Drake: Again, I did not set any fires. I want just as much as anyone to identify the true cause of the fire.

Thorp: Just like O.J., right?

Drake: What?

Thorp: You want civilized discourse, scientific debate. Well, we're lucky, Nathan! Because I know you are a big fan of the black-backed woodpecker and we just happen to have on the line another very knowledgable birdwatcher who takes what we might call some umbrage—a fine civilized word—at your opinions.

Drake: Roger, I'm always happy to talk about woodpeckers. The black-backed have evolved over millions of years to live in burned out forests. You know, it's amazing, some of the beetles they feed on have special heat-sensing organs that allow them to detect a fresh burn from miles away.

Thorp: Nathan, Dr. Heath, hold on. Matty, do we have him on the line? Yes, I think we have you on the line now, are you there?

Heath: I'm here, Roger. Thank you for inviting me back.

Thorp: Let me introduce Dr. LaVonne Heath. He has degrees in biology and forestry from the University of Oregon. He was a wildland firefighter and a smoke jumper for several years before settling down as a city firefighter and then fire chief in several big cities around eastern Washington and Idaho. And now he's put down the fire hose and acts as one of the nation's top independent fire investigators and expert witnesses in fire-related cases.

Heath: Thank you, Roger. I suppose it was really my PhD work at Stanford that allowed me to make that last career transition so I can apply legal concepts and precepts to the whole intersectionality of fire and the economy.

Thorp: Well, Dr. Health, say hello to Nathan Drake.

Heath: Hello, Nathan.

Drake: Hello. Fellow Stanford grad here. Engineering. Water Quality. And Microbiology. PhD.

Heath: Ah.

Drake: Assume you were at the Law School? Or was it the Environmental Studies program? Both excellent.

Heath: Yes. They are.

Thorp: Enough alum chit chat you two. LaVonne, what's your question for Nathan?

Heath: Right. Here's the thing. We all know the black-backed woodpeckers require the burn zone to thrive. No one questions that. But how hot do the fires need to be?

Drake: Yes! Good point. The research is telling us that megafires, which burn ultra-hot, may not in fact be ideal for the black-backed woodpecker.

Heath: A legacy of our old policies of extinguishing all fires.

Drake: Exactly. The black-backed woodpecker prefers nesting at the edges of a burn.

Heath: So the fledglings in that eco-zone can access the lower-severity burn zones and—

Thorp: Whoa, hey, enough geeking out, you two. Now, LaVonne, I understand you are investigating the origins of some of our local fires here in Sahaptin County.

Heath: That's right, Roger. I've been working with local officials to help where I can.

Thorp: And what's our status right now?

Heath: Of course I can't discuss specifics, but let's just say that the early guesses as to origins were never substantiated.

Thorp: No lightning, you mean?

Heath: That's right, Roger. It looks like the Happy Mountain fire was caused by some trees falling on power lines out near the Icicle Creek area.

Thorp: Duh. What we've been saying all along. Eastern Washington Power can't expect to maintain all their lines using illegal labor from Mexico, despite their denials.

Heath: It does appear that the subcontractor's work for E.W.P. was substandard.

Thorp: And yet the Yakima Tree Trim & Removal Company puts out this bullwhack about their quality work. Photos of cleared lines. These falsehoods need to be stopped.

Heath: A tree fell on the line during the windstorm. I've been up there myself. Facts are facts.

Thorp: And the La Likt River string of fires. What are you finding, Dr. Heath?

Heath: It's classic, Roger. A tow chain being dragged by a luxury van.

Thorp: Have they identified the van's owners? Will they be punished?

Heath: We do know who they are.

Thorp: From Seattle, I understand. So, finally, what's the latest on the Rocky Ridge fire?

Heath: Well, as you know, there is a person of interest who was arrested.

Thorp: That's Nathan here.

Drake: I did not set that fire!

Thorp: But the evidence is there.

Drake: I will be proven innocent!

Thorp: LaVonne, what's your professional opinion?

Heath: Everybody has their day in court, Roger. What I'd want to ask Nathan, if I was in court, is this: Why was your bicycle bell, a highly distinctive bell, found at the exact site of the fire's ignition?

Thorp: His bike bell was there?

Drake: That is not public information and—

Thorp: But really Nathan, don't you want to answer that question here on the air once and for all? I mean, how else could it get there?

Drake: As I told you, Roger, Beth and I did have a break-in at our house a few nights before that fire and, now, while I'm not denying I was on my bike up there looking for my dog—

Thorp: Let me get this straight. You're saying, what? That some kid stole your bike ringer and just happened to drop it exactly where the fire started?

Drake: No, I'm just—

Thorp: Or maybe the dog stole your bell and took it up there! Is that your story?

Drake: Penny was actually saving little Brooklyn Novak that afternoon.

Thorp: So the dog's got a good alibi! What's yours? Hold on there, Nate. I see your attorney is standing up and waving his arms—really flagellating pretty good. Ho! Maybe time for you two to have another chat. Matty, time for us to pay the bills again. Let's take a break.

[Music playing: LOUD GUITAR LICKS]

Matty: In La Likt, McCoy's is your hometown gun shop. Guns, ammo, reloading gear, specialty items like silencers, automatic set-ups—we got it all. We'll even help with your transfers from private parties or other dealers. Hunters, homeowners, citizens: Get ready! McCoy's American Firearms and Home Safety, downtown La Likt.

[Music playing: SEARING GUITAR]

Thorp: All righty. We're back and I'm gonna cut to the chase here. Nathan Drake, you've been accused of arson in the first degree. Sparking a fire in a magnificent forest community.

Drake: I did not set that fire. Why would I talk to you if— I mean —

Heath: You know, it's interesting how arsonists frequently return to the scene of the crime. The literature documents this fact.

Thorp: So, I just hope your lawyer here is a good one, Nate. Hope that wife of yours is ready for a little solo time, because that's what—

Drake: You mention my wife one more time and I will hit you with this rock!

Thorp: Wow, let the record show, Nate here is hefting my prize piece of Teanaway serpentine. That rock must weigh a good 15 to 20 pounds.

Drake: My wife has nothing to do with this!

Thorp: True, you're the one who did it. She's a victim like the rest of us.

Drake: Just shut up about her.

Thorp: But Mary Beth Drake doesn't shut up about us does she? She's always writing those nasty stories about local families for that British rag.

Drake: She's doing her job.

Thorp: Like her false narrative about hay subsidies in the Sahaptin Valley. And converting prime rangelands into nonmotorized play parks for city folks.

Drake: All triple sourced, you [BLEEP].

Thorp: My family has grown hay out of Ellensburg for four generations now and—

Drake: So you're a pet food grower, you sanctimonious [BLEEP]. Big [BLEEP]ing deal. Your hay mostly feeds horses owned by rich people in Seattle and Japan. And maybe a few of your buddies who like to play cowboy. Maybe a cow or two, sure, but it's not like you're filling hungry bellies around the world.

Thorp: Well, you may not know it, Drake, being from Seattle, but horses in this community play a vital role in the economy and—

Drake: They did a century ago, Thorp. That's why they're in the Sahaptin County Historical Society museum in downtown E-Burg along with the Model T's.

Thorp: What do you know about horses, you little city [BLEEP].

Drake: So, you're growing pet food for rodeo clowns and rich folks. Don't come crying to me when somebody points out that you're getting ridiculous subsidies from the government you're so fond of criticizing. Or when society decides the public land you've been leasing cheap has a better and more environmentally sustainable use.

Thorp: Gimme that [BLEEP]ing rock you—Ah!

Matty: Watch your headset, Roger!

Thorp: Come and get it, Drake!

Matty: Go get'm, Roger!

Drake: I'm right here, you lying sack of [BLEEP].

Matty: Whoa!

Heath: Whoa!

Drake: I don't want my wife's name coming out of your [BLEEP]ing mouth again, Thorp.

Chapter 13

Beth endures a date

I returned to the cabin from the Bullfrog Quick Stop just in time to clear James Novak off the couch before Nathan arrived home from jail. James was doing okay, considering. He spent most of his time on the couch, wrapped in my grandma's orange-and-pink knit afghan despite the summer heat. He chain-drank coffee while quietly making his way through one of my big books of New York Times crosswords—Saturday puzzles, the hard ones I can't get without turning to the answers in the back of the book. James did them in pen. Every hour or so he'd head outside for a smoke break, and the entire population of the cabin would go jittery, worrying until we heard his step coming back across the creaky floor.

But I needed a little time alone with my husband, so James was going to have to handle a session off couch.

Getting arrested for arson is not supposed to be a lark. As I'd learned from my former colleague Patricia Dylan, convictions can put you away for life if someone gets hurt or enough pricey property gets burnt up. The fire Nathan was suspected of starting was threatening the multimillion-dollar houses at Skylandia, where the most exclusive subdivisions now had private firefighting crews installed on every block. The second homeowners had long ago fled the flames, and the few full-time residents had packed their vehicles with photo albums and insurance papers and headed west toward motels and campgrounds reserved especially for evacuees. Those of us left in La Likt and Patrick choked under clouds of smoke and ash that made the air feel like something you should chew well before swallowing. The Farm and Home sold out of air filters, the Safeway cut its hours, and bears were spotted strolling the main street past Dave's brewery.

Meanwhile, my husband was enjoying the bologna sandwiches served in the county lock-up? For someone who spent so much time sitting in his recliner thinking deep thoughts, Nathan could be frustratingly unconcerned about the potential consequences of his own actions. Or, more recently, his own blog posts. Like a lot of people, he felt empowered by the internet to make pronouncements that he otherwise might keep to himself or at least—when dealing face-to-face—issue more diplomatically. Anyway, I hope that's what was going on. I'd hate to think his recent disinhibitions were the first stages of some horrific early onset dementia. Wasn't he acting strange in other ways recently too? Letting chores go? Chasing after Twyla? Crimany. Given his age, maybe the diagnosis wouldn't even qualify as early onset at this point.

Still, despite all my worries, I felt a weight the size of our massive garage fall from me when Bill dropped Nathan at the cabin's threshold. I wrapped my arms around his neck, burrowed my face into his left shoulder, took a deep sniff—pine trees in the sun always came to mind. I felt a rush of love that made me hold on tight even after he had loosened his grip, a signal that we should step inside, out of view of the Chaney's house. Nathan hated public displays of affection.

"How was your night?" I asked him. "Do you have all of your belongings?"

I know it might not seem like it sometimes, but I've loved Nathan Drake ever since I was 19 years old and spotted him cheerily loping down a high Sierra trail, eyes on the peaks across the valley. That's why I was determined to get him to take this situation seriously. I didn't like the thought of spending the rest of my life riding a bus to some faraway prison one Saturday a month for visiting hours. I don't know why I couldn't just drive to the prison, but that's how the scenario played out in my head.

"Hon," I said, once I'd gotten him settled into his recliner with a beer by his elbow and Penny lying atop his feet. "I'm glad you had a good time in jail, but, you know, getting arrested for arson is very serious."

"I didn't do it, though, so it's not that big of a deal," Nathan said dismissively. He took a long pull on his beer. "This would go really well with bologna," he added, almost to himself.

Was he always a bit out of touch, and I'm just noticing now?

"I know you didn't do it," I said. "But other people don't know that. To them, you're the nutcase who wants to burn down the forest to make the woodpeckers happy."

Nathan shrugged. "The Peckerwood," he said.

"Well, yes." I'd have to remember to tell Nathan I'd scheduled the DeRoux brothers to install a new door and clean up the graffiti. If I waited for Nathan to make a decision on the repair, we'd be staring for months at some weirdo's wish for us to burn in hell. Right now, though, I didn't want to get off topic.

"So, like I said, this is a serious charge. And as much as I love Bill Chaney and appreciate his work for us, I think we need an attorney who specializes in criminal defense."

Nathan drained his beer and sighed happily. "Don't worry about it, Beth. Bill's a fine lawyer, and we'll beat the charges. Technically, I didn't do it."

Technically?

"Innocent people go to jail all the time, Nathan."

A look of uncertainty passed over Nathan's face. He gently nudged Penny off his feet and came over to where I stood leaning against the refrigerator. He slipped his arms around me and pulled me in close. "Thank you for arranging all the bail and getting me out of jail," he said, giving me a kiss on the top of my head. "I know the last couple of days have been hard on you too, and I want you to know you don't have to worry about me going to prison ever again."

After decades of marriage, you think you've heard just about everything come out of your spouse's mouth. Take it from me: you haven't.

*****

It was Saturday and Nathan and I had a date. This in spite of the fact that the whole "date night" phenomenon gives me a hard case of the cringes. The idea that people have to schedule special time to be civil to each other makes me wonder how the human race has managed to reproduce so successfully. All right, that's probably just me. But Nathan and I have been married almost 30 years. Don't make me pretend I'm on a date.

Besides, our date was a trip to the Ellensburg Farmer's Market. Don't get me wrong: Ellensburg's got a great farmer's market, and this time of year the stalls are overflowing with all of the best hot weather fruits and vegetables—your eggplant, your peppers, your squash and tomatoes and stone fruit. But a trip to the market is not something Nathan and I usually prepare for in advance, with expectations attached. It's just that our schedules had been so out of sync, what with my best friend dying and my husband being in jail and all. And since his release on bail, most of our time together had been filled with disagreement over the seriousness of our current position vis a vis potential incarceration.

"Nathan, it's not a parking ticket, it's an arson charge," I'd explain. "It's a felony arson charge."

"Uh huh." His muffled response would reach me from somewhere deep within the snack cupboard, where inevitably he'd be rooting for a pick-me-up. "Bill is talking with the DA and, I guess, some of the investigators. He says not to worry too much."

"Bill is an estate attorney," I'd respond. "He's really good at setting up trusts that totally bypass state taxes. Bypassing 20 years to life in prison? Not his specialty."

"Just trust me, Beth," Nathan would say, emerging from the cupboard with a paw full of mixed nuts. "It's not a problem."

"Maybe not for you. You'll be at the state facility in Monroe. I'll be the one on the outside with a front door that no longer locks."

"That's true," he'd respond, chewing a cashew thoughtfully. "I'm not sure when I'll get around to fixing the door, Beth. And if I do go to prison, it probably makes sense for you to sell and move back to California, closer to your family."

"Why would you even say that, Nathan? I mean, if you didn't have something to do with the fire, why would you even be thinking about that?" I caught myself checking out the backs of his hands for tattoos. Were they raw from vigorous scrubbing or was it just the result of less than diligent moisturizing? By this point, if I was on the jury, I might vote to lock him up.

It didn't help that our tiny cabin was still fully occupied by mammals of varying social skills—Cassie, Nigel, James, the six chimps, the two dogs, Nathan, and me all smashed together in something less than a thousand square feet, not counting the unfinished garage. When they heard that special tone of voice that meant words were about to be exchanged, the dogs usually slunk out of the room, bellies nearly sweeping the boot-beat fir floors. The humans, though, would sometimes try to join in, and their take on Nathan's guilt or innocence wasn't encouraging.

"You think of getting a prison consultant?" James interjected one morning after I'd pointed out Bill Chaney's lack of criminal trial experience. James so seldom spoke that Nathan and I stopped mid-squabble to stare at him. "Buddy of mine told me about it. They can help you choose the facility that best matches up with your needs. Like, if you want a good drug rehab program or the best gym." James eyed my husband. "Or maybe good bathrooms or something."

"Mary Beth!" Nigel gushed over lunch as I was again pointing out that the charge was in fact a felony, and therefore, extremely serious. "You must stop worrying! We can cover Nathan's trial together. And after, I can try to get you on at the paper in London, if things turn out to be as hard for you here as seems likely."

"Being behind bars," Cassie grimly interrupted in the late afternoon as Nathan was assuring me of his upcoming exoneration. She shook her head slowly over her daily Gin & Tonic. "Getting locked up? It's bad. Doesn't matter if you're a chimp like Holly or an arsonist like Nathan."

Add to that the fact that I was spending more time with Nigel than with Nathan and Nathan was spending more time with Twyla than with me, and that's how you find yourself typing "date time" into your calendar app. Mine alerted me to the fun ahead at seven in the morning, bleating me out of a dream that prominently featured mint chocolate chip ice cream. This made me a little crabby, so I got dressed in whatever was laying on the floor next to my side of the bed, scored an unimpeded visit to our only bathroom, and then tiptoed past Cassie's room. I met up with Nathan a few steps later in the kitchen. He was trying to grind beans for coffee without waking James. To our eyes, James seemed to be doing pretty well, but we were aware that on top of losing his mother and nearly losing his daughter, he'd left rehab before the course of treatment had ended.

"I've been through it before," he'd said, trying to reassure us. "In fact, I've been through it twice before. I know what comes next." That this wasn't a particularly encouraging piece of information didn't seem to occur to him. Still, we knew he was having trouble sleeping, and once he achieved that state of bliss, we hated to wake him.

"Is it best to go in short bursts, or just blast away and get it over with?" Nathan whispered, his fingers wiggling indecisively next to the grinder's bright red power button.

I hesitated. "The outcome is bad either way. Why don't we give ourselves a special treat and get coffee out this morning?"

"Indeed! Why not? Seeing as it's our very delightful day together, just we two," Nathan added in his best British accent. He put his palms together under his chin in Nigel's manner, and I had to make that snick-snick-snick sound of a person trying to suppress laughter without actually snorting.

Nothing brings two people together faster than making fun of a third.

By the time we got to Ellensburg, it was well past time for Nathan's midmorning snack. Our county seat had become a prosperous place once the railroad arrived in the 1880s—the financial and market hub for the surrounding ranchers and farmers. And thanks to the inevitable fire that leveled much of the town in the 1890s, Ellensburg's early 20th century buildings are now filigreed and turreted in fire-resistant red brick and cream terra cotta. On farmer's market Saturdays in August, the downtown streets are lined with booths offering every type of local temptation: plums, peaches, the earliest pears and apples from the county's orchards, cherry hand-pies and coffee from the local bakery, and skewers of pasture-raised beef sizzling on a portable grill overseen by a large woman in a battered straw cowboy hat. We ambled by all of it once to check it out, headed through again just in case we'd missed anything, and then eased by once more because now that we'd seen the choices close up, we were absolutely paralyzed by indecision. By the time we started our fourth walk-through, some of the vendors had begun to pack up their stands.

"Tamales Don Chayo," Nathan said, stopping to read the banner posted in front of a particularly busy stand. The name was spelled out in red letters on a white background, with green chilis sprinkled liberally in the background. Below the lettering, a cartoon tamale sporting wide eyes and a bright smile waved its little stick arms at us. Its hands were sheathed in what looked like boxing gloves. "Where have I seen that before?" Nathan asked.

We watched the stand's customers, some coming away with bags bulging with tamales to cook at home and others carrying red-and-white checked paper plates heaped with corn-husk wrapped packets balanced on mounds of plump pinto beans. The scent of garlic and onion made my mouth water.

"I know!" I said. "Tamales Don Chayo! They won a Beard Award last year."

"Beard?"

"Yeah, you know. Awards named for a very influential New York Times writer. They give them to people who make exceptional food. Tamales Don Chayo won last year. I remember it was a big deal because they're a family shop in a small town."

"So, we should try them?" Nathan asked.

"Definitely," I said, joining the line.

"Tamales Don Chayo," Nathan repeated as we inched closer to the booth to place our orders. "I know I've seen that fighting tamale somewhere before." I opened my mouth to explain again about the Beard Award. He held up his hand to stop me. "Not because of the bearded award," he said. "It's something else."

After every couple of orders, a teen-aged girl wearing a red-and-green striped apron and a trucker cap featuring the boxing tamale popped out from the stand to erase another menu item from a white board placed near the front of the line. "Sold out of veg!" she sang. "Still have beef, pork, and chicken." Then, the next time, "Still have chicken and beef."

I was about to lament missing out on the veg tamales when Nathan's rapier-like elbow caught me in the ribs. "I've got it!" he said as I rubbed my side. "The girl! She's Hector Hernandez's daughter."

"Blanking," I said.

"You know, the power company's contractor for tree trimming. Twyla and I met them out in the Icicle drainage, where the Happy Mountain fire started." He scrunched up his face, the better to call up the memory. "Her name's Lucy. Or no, Lindsey!"

At the mention of her name, the girl appeared and wiped "beef" off the menu. "Only chicken left," she said, smiling broadly. "Only chicken for you slowpokes. We're closing soon."

"Lindsey!" Nathan called. "Hey! Over here!" The girl turned toward us, her grin falling into a wary scowl.

"Sir?" she said stonily.

"Maybe you don't recognize me without my binoculars," Nathan said, rolling his fingers into tubes and miming as though he was looking at an ivory billed woodpecker or something similarly extinct. "We met out by Icicle Creek. You and your dad were inspecting the power lines. My friend and I—" He turned toward me. "Not her— this is my wife, Beth—but you remember the younger, blonder woman—"

"Wow," I muttered. "Thanks."

Nathan looked at me distractedly and made as if to pat my head before thinking better of it and sticking his hand in his pocket. "My friend and I were looking for woodpeckers, and we ran into you and your dad. We talked about the fire?"

A trace of a smile returned to Lindsey's face. "Oh yeah," she said. "The woodpecker dude. You were with the reporter who gave me this." She reached into the back pocket of her sloppy jeans and produced a business card. "Nice of you all to take an interest."

"Yes!" Nathan chirped just as a slender woman, her dark hair streaked gray beneath her Don Chayo cap, began letting down the canvas curtain that separated us from the tamales. "Sorry, sold out!" she yelled. "Sold out, folks! Sold out, Lindsey!"

Those of us left in line let out a dismayed sigh—the collective, low-pitched sound reserved for moments of deep disappointment—as the triumphant owner of the last two chicken tamales passed back through the crowd, red-and-white plate held high. One fat guy in biker's leathers yelled, "shit!" and, turning on his steel toes, stomped off toward the grass-fed beef hamburger stand.

I was as distressed as anyone and I must have looked it because Lindsey suddenly took me by the forearm. "Come on," she whispered. "My auntie always saves lunch for the family. You can eat with us."

Behind the tamale stand, Lindsey pulled aside three folding chairs and motioned for us to sit. A moment later, she returned with three plates. "My auntie's special recipe," she said. "Asparagus and pepper jack cheese."

"Your aunt is Tamales Don Chayo?" I asked, sloppily unwrapping a corn husk to reveal the soft, golden masa underneath.

"Yeah, my dad's sister and her family," Lindsey said, balancing the perfect proportion of cornmeal, asparagus, and cheese on her plastic fork. "I help her out on market days, but mainly I work with my papa's business. His customers like to hear an All-American girl accent when they call up, you know?" She brought the fork to her chapped lips and blew on her tamale. "And then, you know, I go to high school, plan for college. I like tamales and I like trees, but not enough to make a career out of either of them."

"What do you want to do, Lindsey?" Nathan asked.

She shrugged, and tilted her head to the right. "My papa wants me to be an engineer." She looked up at us and widened her eyes in comic alarm. "And not even a computer engineer. A civil engineer."

"Everybody's papa wants them to be an engineer," I mumbled, managing a bite. The asparagus held just the slightest crunch, the stalks popping under my teeth and melting into the cheese. I closed my eyes and sighed. "But you," I said when I came to. "Do you have ideas for your future?"

"Oh yeah!" she said. "I have lots of ideas. Like first, I'm going to be rodeo queen this year if it kills me."

Nathan and I exchanged a look.

"What?" she asked, taking in our surprised expressions. "It looks good on my college applications, especially for the East Coast schools." She laughed. "Rodeo queen! Makes the incoming freshman class diverse. And besides, it's about time that we had a Hernandez on the Royal Court, right?" She set her plate next to the legs of her folding chair and looked around until she spotted a bright pink backpack with "Yakima Rodeo" spelled out across the front flap in silver sequins. "I'm already a princess, so if I can just show enough enthusiasm for this darn place between now and the end of the summer, next time you see me I should be wearing the big crown on the front of my cowgirl hat." She extracted a rectangular ticket book from the pack and waved it at us. "Do you have your rodeo tickets yet?" she asked. "Help a poor Mexican girl realize the American Dream!"

"Cash?" I whispered to Nathan, who shifted left to fetch his wallet from his back pocket.

"I shouldn't be so cynical about the rodeo, or the town," Lindsey said apologetically as Nathan handed over a fistful of twenties in exchange for two single-day passes. "I do sincerely want to be queen, and most people here are decent. But it only takes a few nasty ones to make an impression."

"Like the ones saying stuff about your dad and how the Happy Mountain fire started?" Nathan asked.

"Uh huh," she said, stuffing the ticket book back into her sparkly pack, then tossing it away with a fake shudder. "Thorp and his dudes —I can't take much more of those guys. I want to get my cousins together and go out to their so-called studio. Maybe break a little equipment while I inform them of a few essential truths." She grinned at us, then sighed. "But my papa's head would literally explode if I even joked about that." She paused. "Well, not literally explode, I guess, but he would not like it." She emphasized the last five words as if they were separate sentences. "And anyway, they're saying stuff about you, too, you know."

"We know," I said.

"Lies," Nathan said.

She nodded grimly. "Yeah, I know all about Thorp and his super-patriot buddies. It's part of the reason I'm going to be a lawyer. I tell Papa, think of all the people I could help if I knew how to use the law, right? Somebody else can build the bridges. Maybe my baby sister."

"What do you know about Thorp?" I asked.

She leaned toward me. "Same things you do, if you think about it. Comes from an old Sahaptin Valley family. Big fish in a little pond for decades. But now that the younger generation has departed for greener pastures the Thorps are out of the hay business." She smiled at the pun. "Sold the family car dealership. No more Thorps on the City Council or in the Rodeo Royalty. Things going from bad to worse."

"The world is changing around Roger Thorp," I said. "I can understand he doesn't like that much."

"Yeah," she responded, "But tough shit. Things change, sometimes for the better, old man."

"So he starts a videocast just to vent about making Sahaptin County great again?"

She frowned and reclaimed her plate of tamales. "Yeah, but not just to vent. To get some of that power back. And now that he has a little pull around here again, he's hungry for national exposure. For sure he's not satisfied being the Voice of Colockum Ridge, because who knows where that is, right? He wants to be the voice of a national movement. How to do that? Maybe start by capitalizing on the fires? Get a little national attention by suggesting they're started by a fatal combination of immigrants and arson?"

"You're saying the fires are good for Thorp," I said.

"Of course they're good for Thorp. And other people, too." She nodded and leaned back in her chair, gesturing with her fork. "It's not climate change, it's illegal Mexicans cutting trees into power lines so they can distract law enforcement from their main business, which is drug running or people smuggling or some other anti-American action."

She shook her head in disgust and continued. "It's not what the dry winters are doing to the forests, it's the liberal elite van-lifers, dragging chains and sparking fires because they look down on the decent people who have been here all of their lives."

She turned to Nathan. "It's not the wave after wave of excessive heat, it's that whacked-out environmentalist woodpecker lover, looking to open up more space for birds. His stuff was found at the ignition site. Plus somebody saw him set that fire, right?"

Nathan gazed at her, open-mouthed. "But who believes all that?" he asked.

"Plenty of people," she said grimly, gazing at the happy farmer's market crowd heading home with their bags of tomatoes, their boxes of berries, their kettle corn and raspberry pies. "Maybe even I believe it. There's definitely enough evidence against you."

She nodded to our right. "For sure, that guy over there believes it. He's been watching me all day."

We followed her gaze, just in time to see a slender man near the Polish Dog cart pivot and then dart away through the shuffle of market-goers.

"Nathan!" I said. "It's The Doppelgänger."

Chapter 14

Nathan goes down to the river

Twyla arrived just as Beth was leaving to meet Nigel. Those two were off on some top secret British special assignment, as usual.

"You and Nathan going birdwatching again?" Beth asked—somewhat cattily, I thought. Her canvas school bag was slung over her shoulder and her eyes were fixed on the cabin's front door, which I had jimmied just enough to allow pedestrian access.

"Actually, I'd like to talk with you, Beth," Twyla said.

"Just on my way out," she replied. "You two have fun."

"It's important," Twyla said, holding out her arm to stop my wife. "Listen, I know you're reporting on the fires. And I know you're upset about my sudden interest in Nathan."

"Oh, who wouldn't be interested in Nathan?" Beth said, throwing a look back at me. I was standing in in the middle of the living room in my sweatpants and a threadbare T-shirt from the Stanford Microbiology Department softball team. I held a half-roll of Ritz crackers in my hand. Penny stood at my side, both of us aiming apprehensive looks toward the scene at the doorstep, as if a fight might break out at any moment.

"Here's the deal," Twyla said, letting Beth's barely disguised vitriol roll right off her. "I'm an undercover fire investigator. My assignment is to integrate within the community and identify arson suspects."

Beth stared at Twyla.

"Suspects including your husband."

Beth looked back at me again. "You knew about this, Nathan?"

"Not until Bill told me when he got me out of jail," I said. "Never even heard of undercover fire investigators before this."

Beth, the gears still turning, looked back to Twyla.

"We're fairly sure Nathan had nothing to do with the fire," Twyla said, her arm finally lowered to allow Beth an escape option. "Muriel said so from the start, and I've already talked with the DA, but we still need to chase down a few leads."

"I was never a serious suspect, Beth," I said, happy to have the news out in the open. "But the DA and sheriff were getting heat from Thorp so they needed to make the arrest. Bill and I couldn't say anything when we finally found out, which was just before my release." I grinned and reached toward her, offering a Ritz as a peace token.

Beth stood as still as a coiled snake, positioned between Twyla and me. After a few long seconds, she said in a conversational tone, "So you and Bill couldn't say anything. Why not?" She turned quickly and stared straight at Twyla. "Of course, you expert investigators know best, but arresting him even though you don't think he's a credible suspect, releasing him on bail, then keeping it quiet? That seems like a pretty dicey legal move." She shrugged, then turned back to me, smiling sweetly. "I mean, I'm only the wife, I know, but does that seem at all questionable to you, Nathan?"

Uh oh.

"Lock you up for no real reason," Beth continued, smile gone, voice rising. "But on no account should you tell me that. No, have me run around, worried sick and raising bail money." She dropped her bag to the floor. I heard the sound of glass breaking. Pasta salad for lunch?

"I put our house up as collateral, for God's sake!" Beth yelled.

When she put it that way, it did seem a little suspicious. "We'll get the money sorted out," I said uneasily. "We certainly won't lose the house."

"We needed some time, Beth," Twyla replied, coldly professional. "Let some other suspects relax and slip up because we had a person of interest in custody. And we had plenty of evidence to hold Nathan. Circumstantial evidence, yes, and now the investigation has advanced. Our attention is elsewhere."

Beth shifted her weight forward to the balls of her feet and clenched her fists. I should have warned Twyla not to go official on her. She's got a problem with authority. But next she turned her blazing eyes on me. If my sweat pants suddenly had caught fire, I wouldn't have been surprised.

"Look," Twyla continued, her tone warming, "Muriel and I appreciate your leads. The work of Nigel and Penny, of course. Wow. Unbelievable. And now we're at a point where you should know about my real role here. That's it. That's why I'm here today."

"Gee," Beth spat. "Thanks."

"Maybe best not to tell Nigel," Twyla added.

"No," I blurted. "Of course not."

"So, your son," Beth said. "Does he always tag along on your assignments?"

"Glenn. It's Ben actually," she answered. "On assignment from Whitman County Fire District. Twenty-five years old. Wife and a baby girl at home."

"Glenn's not yours?" I asked.

Beth and Twyla both looked at me. A double-barreled silent assessment.

"And for what it's worth, Beth," Twyla continued, waiting until she had secured full eye contact with my wife, "Nathan was always a perfect gentleman with me."

"Oh, I'm sure," Beth said. "He's always so generous. With strangers."

"And with your permission," Twyla went on, "I'd like to recruit him again today for another little birdwatching trip."

This was news to me.

"It seems a little late to be asking my permission for anything," Beth said. She sucked in a long breath and blew it out slowly. Then she did it again. Her deep breathing exercises. A good sign.

"Is it safe for him to be walking around?" she asked, shrugging a shoulder toward me. "After his interview with Thorp, I mean, seems like all the wrong people will know he's out."

"Well," said Twyla, giving me a long look. "It might be useful to see who tries to bother him."

"So, he's bait?" asked Beth. "Again?"

Twyla shrugged her shoulders. "Kind of, yeah. I'll be with him all day, though. Got a lead on the owner of the red truck."

*****

I felt foolish now being alone with Twyla. Had my feelings for her involved more than a common interest in birds? More than an instinct to help a new neighbor and her son integrate into what could be, for all the talk of small-town friendliness, a community that's hard to crack?

Of course they had. I'm only a man. She was an extremely attractive woman who shared my interests and, despite my age, appreciated my company. Her attention was totally flattering and, in retrospect, I had fallen for her like a schoolboy.

In fact, I reflected while driving the Subaru east toward the Columbia River, the last time I felt this mortified about a girl was in high school when Susie Vanderkamp dumped me for my best friend Todd Reynolds. Or, also in high school, when I had picked up a leather-skirted hitchhiker in my family's Plymouth and she had been so nice, asking personal questions, laughing at my quirky jokes, touching my thigh. Only when she asked if I wanted a date did it dawn on my adolescent brain that she was a prostitute.

But at least it was fairly easy to avoid Susie at high school. And I dropped off the nice hitchhiker soon after declining her offer, never to see her again.

There was no avoiding Twyla. These are the indignities that old men must bear.

Once we reached the river, we were going to cross and head up to the Ancient Lakes area, just south of Quincy. About an hour's drive. I locked in the cruise control and put on my most stoic demeanor, letting Twyla steer the conversation.

"Thanks again for agreeing to this," she said. "Two birders with binoculars, especially a couple, are always more invisible than a solo."

"I'd like to help out," I said.

She was attempting to shield her eyes and the phone in her lap from the sun, which poured in through the windshield. Squinting hard, she used a navigation app to follow the progress of a red dot that represented the truck we'd seen at the Bountiful warehouse.

"It's still parked near the Ancient Lakes. At least, I think it is," Twyla said. "If the air tag didn't fall off on those rough roads. We can always pick him up where he lives, but much better to catch him in the act at the new grow house."

Twyla explained that the red truck's license plate number easily pegged the owner as a former Bonneville Power lineman living in Wenatchee. Only 42 years old, he retired early and somehow managed to own two spectacular mountain homes—one outside Wenatchee, the other in the Methow Valley—plus a recently acquired 500-acre choice spread on the Teanaway River.

She reached up and slammed down the Subaru's sun flap. Then she struggled to press my Washington road atlas up against her side window, keeping it pinned with her shoulder, to block the sun. "I don't know why people bother to grow illegally, inside," she fumed, "when pot is legal these days and the damn sun never stops shining."

I didn't offer up any speculation.

"You know, Nathan," she said, "just to clear the air. I really did enjoy spending time with you. Talking about your ideas. Hiking up in the Icicle Canyon. The birding was amazing. I wasn't entirely faking it."

"You were doing your job," I said. "I respect that. You did a good job."

"Sometimes I confuse myself about where my job ends and my real life begins. Occupational hazard. I could've had you locked up even sooner—for your own protection, you know. Anyway, you're a nice guy. Fun."

"Well, thanks, Twyla." I said. "Is that your real name?"

"Don't you like it?" she teased, flopping her braid over her shoulder.

*****

The east side of the Columbia River is Ice Age Flood country. About 15,000 years ago, a glacial dam on Lake Missoula broke and a massive torrent roared out of what is now Montana and raced across the whole Columbia River drainage. The cataclysmic flood scoured deep channels in the old lava plains as it rushed toward the Pacific. This happened over and over, at least 25 times in two thousand years, carving out what is today an eerie land of dark rock coulees and basalt plateaus known collectively and with an appropriate note of rawness as the channeled scablands.

The Ancient Lakes are a chain of dinky potholes gouged into these chocolate-brown scablands. From the recreation area's parking lot, the main trail drops past waterfalls, which in short order feed the lakes and then debouch into the mighty Columbia River itself. But Twyla and I didn't take that trail. Instead, we stayed high on the basalt bluffs and, binoculars in hand, headed for the red dot, which

Twyla's phone still insisted was near the fruit warehouse in the distance.

Threading our way through sagebrush steppe, we angled toward the string of high-voltage towers that ran more or less parallel to the river. Moving north on the cleared ground under the transmission towers would take us directly to the warehouse.

I was sorry to be missing out on the birding here. The grouse, flycatchers, sparrows, thrashers, and, of course, the hawks. All my bird friends who may not survive here much longer. The Cascade forests to the west steal the public's attention, but loss of this sagebrush sea to rangeland fires, invasive plants, and development is equally dramatic.

Immersed as I was in this gloomy line of thought, I was grateful when we finally got close to the warehouse. The red dot on Twyla's phone, we could now confirm through our binoculars, was indeed the red truck. It was parked between the cinderblock warehouse and a derelict electrical substation that was surrounded by a rusting chain-link fence. Was this an old step-down station to send hydro energy to nearby towns or industries such as—what? Refrigerated warehouses? Aluminum smelters? Potato processing plants?

"You with me, Nathan?" asked Twyla. "Need to be on the same page."

"Gotcha. You're my beautiful young wife. We're crazy about the Greater Sage Grouse. But we neglected to bring along any drinking water."

"That'll do," she said. "And remember, I've got a warrant and my sidearm if he gets nasty."

We marched up to the warehouse, close to the red truck's parking spot. A powerful vibratory thrum came from inside, like a generator or an AC or filtration unit. We stood in the shade along the north side of the building and considered the steel door.

"Let's knock and see if anyone can help us," Twyla said in a loud voice.

I pounded on the metal with the side of my fist—boom, boom, boom.

"Hello," I yelled. "Anybody in there? We could use some water out here."

No response.

Again my boom, boom, boom.

"What can I help you with?" A deep voice came from the other side of the truck. "Private property down here, you know."

He had on a white hardhat and a Ben Davis striped shirt, the type with the little ape face embroidered on the pocket. He carried a loop of thick electrical wire over his shoulder and a couple wrenches in his hand. To all appearances, he was just returning from the substation. He'd popped open the toolbox on the far side of his truck and was stashing his gear.

"Hey there," said Twyla. "Yeah, sorry to bother you, but my husband and I were just out birdwatching. Got a little off course and realized we didn't have our water bottles. Saw your truck. Any chance you can help us out with some water?"

"Sure thing," he said, reaching into the cab and pulling out two unopened plastic bottles, liter size. "Kind of warm. But. That do you?"

Mr. Electric didn't seem like a pot grower to me. But maybe I'd read too many stories about off-the-grid dreadlock types in Mendocino County.

"What's up with the substation today?" I asked, twisting open the bottled water. I could see a heavy electrical line drooping from the substation to the rear of the warehouse.

"Just maintenance, you know," he said. He seemed to be sizing us up. Maybe because he felt nervous. Maybe because my beautiful wife was married to such a doofus.

"I guess this building is some kind of, what, fruit storage?" asked Twyla, all innocence. "Looks like it's hooked up to the substation there."

"That'd be correct, ma'am," he said, eyeing us both more carefully. "I should be heading back. You all set for water?"

"Yeah. We're good," said Twyla, one moment crouching to stow her new water bottle in her daypack and the next standing with a gun in one hand and a piece of paper in the other.

"But I'm afraid I have a warrant for your arrest, Tom Write. I'm Twyla Larson, fire investigator for the State of Washington. Please put your hands on the hood of the truck."

Twyla handcuffed the big man to his truck rack while I found two pistols, one in each toolbox. When Twyla explained why he was being detained, he just laughed mildly and hung his head. When Twyla asked for the key to the warehouse, he sighed, laughed again, and said, "It's open. See for yourself."

The heavy door swung open and a gush of cool air came pouring out, along with a high-pitched whirring. The large interior was NOT filled with a vibrant green forest of pot plants under blinding grow lights. The air was NOT saturated with hothouse humidification. The room was NOT overpowered by a skunky scent of cannabis.

It took both Twyla and me a stupefied second or two, standing there in the doorway, to dislodge those preconceptions from our minds and replace them with what really met our eyes: computer servers, racks and racks of them, floor to ceiling, humming and pulsing, stubbled with short loops of black wire, and greedy for the gouts of cooling air pushed from the hulking AC units positioned all around the periphery of the room.

"What the hell is this?" Twyla said, stepping even closer to me to be heard. "Part of the substation?"

"Looks more like one of those bitcoin mining operations to me," I said. "Cryptocurrency? I read they're quite the deal around

Wenatchee. They need to be situated close to the cheap hydro power so they can run all the calculations, to create new bitcoins, I guess."

"So, is this, like, legal?" Twyla asked.

"You're the law," I said. "Maybe the electrician can enlighten us."

"Whatever it is, it sure runs hot and sucks power. You can see how it might've gotten out of control up Icicle Creek."

We were backing out, intending to question the guy attached to his truck, when I got a whiff of smoke.

"Smell that?" I asked. "Something on fire in there?"

We hurried into the warehouse and around the computer towers to the back of the room. At a cheap desk in the far corner sat The Italian. Bare chested, barefooted, skinny jeans, he was leaning back in a mesh swivel chair, calmly smoking a cigarette. On his desk was a distinctive MS cigarette packet, like the one we'd found near the ignition point of the Happy Mountain fire. A video feed of the warehouse exterior played across his computer screen. We could see Mr. Electric cuffed to his bumper, sitting on his tailgate in the slanting afternoon light.

"I told Write it no work," The Italian yelled over the racket of the AC.

All subsequent dialogue was carried on, necessarily, at 200 percent of normal volume.

"We have a warrant for the arrest of your friend out there," Twyla yelled back, "for starting the Happy Mountain fire."

"Yeah? He should be arrest for crap wiring."

"Who are you working for?" asked Twyla.

"Working for the blockchain, baby," he said, now giving Twyla a good top-to-bottom look. He crushed out his smoke in a bowl-like glass insulator on his desk.

"You've been around La Likt for four or five months now," I said. "I see you walking around downtown."

"Your transit sucks," he said, finally taking note of me. "Hard to get around."

"So, your boss?" Twyla tried again. "We really need to check on the permits for this operation."

"Il permesso!" he yipped at 400 percent volume. "Buona fortuna!"

"A name and number," Twyla said more sternly.

"I cannot," said The Italian, seeming genuinely sad as he slid another cigarette from the pack and stared at Twyla's chest. "I don't know any names but Write. Subcontract." After lighting the cigarette he added: "I get paid for certain duties at certain times. Only work with electrician."

Mention of the electrician made all three of us look again at the monitor. Tom Write was screaming and hopping around on one foot out there in the hot setting sun.

"I pull the plug," said The Italian, cigarette dangling between his lips. He sat up straight, thrust his bare chest forward, and tapped on his keyboard.

"I go back to Bologna."

*****

The rattlesnake had only nipped the Vibram sole of Mr. Electric's heavy boot. But that brush with a venomous reptile while shackled to his own truck seemed to be some kind of final indignity for the electrician. An hour later, he was singing like a sagebrush sparrow at sunset.

It would be another two hours before the sheriff arrived along with Twyla's full investigative unit. Twyla and her team eventually spent nearly the whole night under their bright klieg lights, exploring and securing the server farm and its illegally tapped power line.

But before all the crowds arrived, our little foursome drove the electrician's truck up the hill and parked it next to the Subaru. We sat around the back of the truck, drinking bottled water and watching the sun go down over the Columbia and the eastern slopes of the Cascades. Nighthawks and bats pierced the darkening sky. The whole story spilled from the lips of The Italian and the electrician. It wasn't so much an interrogation as a twin-throated road-to-Damascus conversion.

Their story included the name and phone number of a mysterious Canadian, who supposedly brainstormed the whole WorkCoin operation. Her name was considered by one and all to be a fake and the phone was likely a burner. But it was a start, and Twyla was already discretely working contacts as the two songbirds continued their story.

Mr. Electric admitted to using his skills as a former electrical technician with Bonneville Power to tap illegally into the Ancient Lakes substation. He also 'fessed up to his handiwork as the source of the fire at the Bountiful warehouse.

"That little fire whore hired by Thorp told us how to cover it up," he said.

"You mean LaVonne Heath?" I asked. "The private fire investigator?"

"An expert witness," chimed in Twyla. "He had access to all the fire investigation debriefings. He's probably the one who leaked info to Thorp."

"What a weasel," the electrician spat. "Talk about a gun for hire. That guy helped hide our burn and then set up the Mexican line crew."

"Ho boy, got that right," chuckle-snorted Twyla. She had undone a couple buttons on her shirt and was taking long sloppy pulls off her Evian as if it was her fourth Budweiser. I wondered if she had already taken the electrician aside and hinted at a deal. The guy was a gusher of information and I could tell Twyla didn't want to staunch the flow.

"Anyway, the Canadian said we needed to ramp up fast before the whole crypto thing crashed," the electrician continued. "I told her we shouldn't try to squeeze any more out of that Icicle line. There's only so much load you can tap before it gets unpredictable."

"We needed more power for the new I.C.O.," said The Italian, his impressive chest now residing within a crisp white dress shirt, untucked, above his jeans and brown Milano loafers.

"I.C.O.?" asked Twlya. The Italian and Twlya were both leaning against the open tailgate of the red truck and had been chain smoking since sunset.

"Initial coin offering," he said in a gentle, teacherly tone. "We create the currency and then sell, sell, sell."

"I don't understand how bitcoin works," said Twyla.

"No one does, baby. No one does. It's the beauty."

"So how did the Canadian find you for this work?" she asked Mr. Electric as she accepted another cigarette from the accommodating Italian.

"Roger Thorp gave him my name," said the electrician. "Roger knew me from his son's high school football team in Ellensburg. Called me out of the blue with this 'potentially lucrative side gig,' he called it."

"He have skin in the game himself?" I asked, already knowing the answer.

"Oh yeah. Big time. There's a reason why he pumps WorkCoin on his radio shows. Also why he hires a private investigator to shift the blame for the Happy Mountain fire."

"And you?" Twyla said softly to the elegant Italian beside her. "How'd you get wrapped up in all this?"

"Ah, fate," he said, turning his eyes up to the star-crowded sky. "Schoolmate from Bologna now in Seattle. Start-up thing. Spin-off. Friend of friend. I come to La Likt."

Twyla put a hand on his shoulder.

"And the young Italian's fortune was lost," he added as if reading the last line of a book.

*****

I remained with The Italian, Mr. Electric, and a sheriff's office rookie while the full investigation team did their poking around down at the substation and the warehouse. We all nodded off a bit in the seats of the truck's double cab.

By the time Twyla returned, the first rosy hints of dawn were appearing in the east.

She was planning to ride back with Sheriff Peters for a more formal interrogation of our suspects, but as The Italian and Mr. Electric were being loaded into the back of a cruiser, a report erupted from the radio.

"Wildfire reported in hills approximately five miles north of Ellensburg. Crews dispatched."

Twyla stepped away to make a call to Muriel.

"It's not big but Muriel says it's just north of Thorp's Colockum Ridge place," she said as she speed-walked toward the Subaru. "I told her what our boys said about Thorp."

"Beth told me that Walt and Eleanor Lundquist own property just north—" I was alarmed to discover that I was wheezing slightly as I trotted after her. "North of Thorp's place."

"The couple with the chain-dragging RV?" She stopped, thank God, and stared at me.

"Yeah, but apparently somebody hooked that chain to their RV after they drove down the river road."

"A setup?"

"A setup."

"Thorp?"

"Some guy in a Camaro. Who looks like me. I think I know him, actually."

"Good thing you were with me all that day, sweetie."

"It's a good alibi all right."

"So, this fire?"

"Likely not a coincidence."

"Want another chance to crown Thorp with a big old rock?"

*****

The Subaru was climbing the grade up from the Columbia River crossing when Twyla's phone chirped and she put it on speaker.

I heard the agitated voice of Hector Hernandez.

"It's Lindsey," he shouted. "My daughter. Man with a SA-15 just forced his way into our house and took her away. White guy in a red QAnon hat." Twyla took in a sharp gulp of air. Her hand went to the sidearm at her ribs as if to check on its wellbeing. She took a few breaths before she spoke.

"Hello?" Hector said, panic in his voice. "You're going to help me, right?"

"What do the police say?" Twyla asked, trying to keep her voice professional.

"I called you," Hernandez said, his voice rising even higher. "I don't trust police, here or in Mexico. They're always looking for an excuse to shake down my whole crew, search my business. I can't afford to be out of work. I've been calling you instead."

"Hector, this isn't something we can wait around on," Twyla said. "Do you know the man?"

"That's why I called you. He looked like the guy Lindsey and I saw with you up Icicle Creek that day."

Twyla looked at me wide-eyed. "Shit," she said, under her breath. "Hector, I think I know who you mean. Did he say anything?"

"Said I need to stop spreading lies about the Happy Mountain fire. He was mad about what I told you when we talked that day. He said Lindsey was talking too much, too."

"That's it?"

"Told me to go back to Mexico. Drove Lindsey off in a Camaro. Bright orange."

"Hector, we've got to get the police on this," Twyla told him. "I've got a lead on the man you saw, but we don't have time to waste. Hang up and call the police. Give them my number. Do it now!" She ended the call and looked at me, shaken. "You up for this, partner?" she asked.

Once we cleared the long climb up from the river, the Subaru roared west along the empty interstate. A powerful tailwind off the scablands launched us toward the Sahaptin Valley at nearly 110 miles per hour. On a sweeping curve just past Ryegrass Mountain, a semi carrying Hermiston watermelons had tipped and lost its load all over the highway. No cops on the scene yet. The driver, standing on the shoulder with a phone to his ear, looked okay. We slowed and briefly rattled along the rocky median to dodge the ponderous fruits, then accelerated again—the red dawn filling my rearview above the minefield of escaped melons. We exited at the town of Kittitas and headed north toward Colockum Ridge.

Part 4: The Colockum Ridge Fire

Chapter 15

Beth meets her nemesis

I'll admit the whole thing with Fire Investigator Tootsie Pop threw me. It had been a hard enough morning without having to hear all about how Twyla had my husband arrested for her own convenience.

Gee thanks, Twy! Next time, maybe you can get him a more permanent spot in the state prison. I hear the bathrooms are nicer.

But forget about the Bond Girl. At least she's paid to lie and keep state secrets. Why on earth would my husband fail to tell me he'd been jailed not as an arsonist, but to somehow help in the investigation? Why would he let me go two days worrying about his legal representation? Why would he feel no need to set my mind at ease during our "date" at the farmer's market?

It was a good thing I was in a hurry to meet Nigel or I would have said some things that'd make Nathan yearn for the good old days in the custody of Sahaptin County Corrections.

Look, I knew Nathan wasn't much of a talker when I married him. The son of a CIA agent, he got used to keeping secrets early, and his way of avoiding unpleasantness is to simply never mention anything unpleasant, even to me. But I thought we'd made progress the last time we found ourselves in trouble due to his silences. This time, I knew, he was under the influence of that Twinkie Twyla, who told him everything needed to be hush-hush-double-hush. But still. It was upsetting to discover he still didn't trust me with important information.

I'd have to deal with it later. Today Nigel and I were on the trail of The Doppelgänger. Usually, I would have talked to Muriel about the man's suspicious behavior on the night the La Likt River fires started, but I'd tried that once and her angry response still stung. Also, I wanted to ask The Doppelgänger a couple of questions about bike bells and the Rocky Ridge fire ignition point, so I needed to get to him before law enforcement did.

All Nigel and I really knew about The Doppelgänger was, number one, he looked a hell of a lot like Nathan; number two, he might drive an early 2000s Camaro; and, number three, he was one of Roger Thorp's fanboys. So we decided to pay a visit to the Voice of Colockum Ridge. Maybe Thorp could flush out my husband's lookalike for us. Nigel wanted to call first and make an appointment, but I argued that the element of surprise would work in our favor. If Thorp did know The Doppelgänger, what would stop him from telling our target that it might be time to pack the Camaro and move along? I leashed up Penny and waited in front of the cabin for Nigel's Dreadnought to hove into view.

He was late and characteristically unapologetic. "I have some business to take care of before we get to Thorp's worldwide broadcasting center," he said. "Won't be a minute."

And so I sat in the parking lot of the Sno-Cap Motel, listening to Nigel give his "think like a monkey" spiel to a radio reporter back home in the UK. After that came somebody from Der Spiegel and another from the New York Times. Nigel gave me a shrug, as if to say, "Can I help that I happen to be a hero?" and took another call.

"You could at least mention Penny," I said between NPR and the BBC. My pup in the rear seat thumped her tail at the mention of her name. "You could mention Cassie's chimp sanctuary. Maybe get her a few new donors."

"Sorry, darling," he said, giving me a sweet little pout. "I'd do these interviews in my room, but it's the damn interstate highway on the other side of the wall—ruins the audio, the podcasters say." He grinned and brought his palms together just under his chin in a familiar gesture of delight. "The Dreadnought, you know, is absolutely soundproof. I love that about your massive automobiles. No interruption from the outside world at all once you're behind the wheel."

By the time we finally pulled onto Thorp's washboard road, it was late in the evening and dark blue clouds had massed over the pass behind us. Maybe precipitation this time, the forecasters said. The sage-covered ridge hid from us in deep lavender shadows and the air smelled of dust and coming rain. Nigel pulled the Dreadnought up to the chain-link fence surrounding Thorp's compound. The gate was closed and looped shut with a length of shiny silver chain fastened by a large padlock. Old school, I thought, until I spotted the cameras mounted on basalt columns either side of the gate.

"Perhaps they're not home at present," Nigel said, "but I get the distinct sense someone is watching us."

"Cameras," I said, pointing to the devices. Their red electronic eyes bored into us like lasers. Maybe they were lasers. I didn't have much experience with surveillance.

"So, what now?"

"Ehm, I think we park facing downhill and approach on foot."

"Last time they had guns," I reminded him. "And there's that fence. I'm not so keen on flapping around on top like a plastic shopping bag in a stiff breeze. Makes it too easy for them to shoot first and call it trespassing later."

"In that case, Mary Beth, you should have called them before we arrived so we wouldn't be outside a locked gate," Nigel spat. "Though, oh yes! Now I remember! That would have tipped them off. We could have caused The Doppelgänger to run, seeing as somehow we're quite threatening."

We could have gone on happily bickering like this for hours, but the front door of the house suddenly opened wide and a lean figure stepped out onto the concrete stoop.

"Thorp," Nigel said.

"Himself," I answered.

The Voice of Colockum Ridge scurried down the dusty driveway toward us, waving his arms in a "come on in" fashion. He reminded me of nothing so much as an elderly golden retriever, and I wondered what had become of the snarling attack dog I'd seen at the fire meetings.

"If it isn't the man who thinks like a monkey!" Thorp yelled in our direction. He made a show of taking a key from the front pocket of his Wrangler jeans and twisting it into the padlock on the fence. The big gate swung open, and Nigel piloted the SUV to a berth just short of the front door. On the right side of the house, snug against the stucco, sat an orange Camaro.

"Careful, Nigel."

"We'll stay in the car," he said. "Like last time."

The suddenly spritely Thorp caught up to us and rapped on the driver's side window. Nigel nudged it down two or three inches.

"Been trying to reach you and here you are, the man of the moment! Seek and ye shall find, right?" said Thorp, hooking his fingers over the window as if he could force it lower. "I don't believe we've met, Nigel, but I'd love to set up a show with you. Talk about how you got past those government jumbucks and found the little girl when they couldn't. Saved her from the chimp and the fire both. You're a hero to all of us out here on the frontlines, man! Why'nt you come in?"

He was on the verge of turning back toward the house when he spotted me. "Oh, and it's The Peck—Uh, it's Drake's wife! Betty, right? Enjoyed having your husband on the show the other day. His is a unique perspective." He boomed out a rapid "ha ha ha!" that seemed to get stuck in the upper part of his throat as a sudden gust of wind nearly toppled him.

While Nigel and I had been discussing who was at fault for the locked fence and whether either of us would be able to scale it, the temperature outside of the Dreadnought had dropped 20 degrees, the way it can on the edge of the high desert when the weather's about to change. Now the SUV gently rocked in a shower of grit mixed with miniature snowballs. Penny sat up and gave a short warning yip.

"Looks like we might get a storm after all," Thorp said, removing a brown and white plaid handkerchief from a rear pants pocket and wiping his eyes and mouth. "Anyway, welcome to you, too, Betty."

"Why, thank you," Nigel said. "Thank you so much. I'd be happy to be on your show, truly I would." He grimaced. "Yes. Let's definitely find a place on the schedule for that experience. But right now, we've got, ehm, other commitments." He glanced at me.

"Mr. Thorp," I began.

"Roger," he interrupted.

"Right," I said. "We were hoping to get in touch with a gentleman we think you know. We've heard him talk at the community fire meetings, and we've found his take on firefighting very interesting. Thing is, we don't know how to reach him, and we were hoping you can help."

"Who is he?"

"That's just it," Nigel said. "We don't know his name, but he looks like—"

"That fella coming out of the house?" Thorp said. Behind him, The Doppelgänger walked down the drive, rifle hunched under one shoulder and Lindsey Hernandez tucked under the other.

Thorp grinned at us. "Think you all better come inside," he said.

Chapter 16

Nathan receives a vision

We pulled into the little town of Kittitas just as the fleet of sirens arrived off the interstate from the opposite direction. Taking advantage of the town's wide main street—you could turn a 787 in that street—we let the county fire trucks, Forest Service engine crews, and police cars scream past. Then we followed the red-light parade up the hill toward the sunrise-lit mushroom cloud sprouting on the ridge.

"But we're on our way right now," Twyla screamed into her phone.

"Wait for the sheriff," I heard Muriel respond. "He'll have the warrant to search Thorp's place."

"But that could take forever, Muriel. The girl might be in there."

"We've got to do this right."

"All right," Twyla said reluctantly. "We'll wait. There's a pull-out along the creek below his place. We'll park there and hike up to the house to scope it out. We'll be all set when the sheriff arrives."

We continued uphill, negotiating the final series of 90-degree turns typical of farm roads, crossing under the double row of electrical transmission lines, and finally turning onto the rutted track that led to Thorp's place. The fire trucks took a different road, and we could see their dust trail as they closed in on the smoke plume.

The hillside we ascended had burned some ten years ago. About half the blackened pine and Douglas fir snags still stood.

"This was one of my first fires," Twyla said as we bumped up the road. She was fidgeting with her gun, repeatedly checking the clip, and moving the pistol from hand to hand to lap to holster. "We knocked it down in a week. But there was a snafu with the permits for salvage logging. The delay allowed a blue-stain fungus to grow on the pines. It ruined the logs. No lumber. No jobs. Pissed off locals and county commissioners."

She sure seemed chatty, considering where we were headed. Maybe the trick, I thought, is to distract yourself. "Why was there a delay?" I asked.

"Conservation groups. Maybe some of your woodpecker friends."

"Well, salvage logging done right can be part of the solution," I offered. "Especially with this type of overgrown crap."

"Yep. You think this was forest 200 years ago? No way. Native grasses. What exactly are we preserving here? Sometimes even a lying egomaniac like Thorp can be right."

"Hate to say it, but you're right about that."

"Problem is, he's 99 percent wrong," she hissed, suddenly sounding very agitated. "And he's a lying egomaniac."

At least we were thinking about Thorp again. Twyla leaned back and placed a hand over her chest like she was measuring her pulse at its source. She was taking deep breaths and I thought her eyes were closed, but after a minute of silence, the hand flew out and pointed to a pullout where I turned off and tucked the Subaru behind some scrub pines. She immediately opened the door and puked.

After hocking a few loogies, she got out, leaned on the side of the Subaru, and wiped her mouth with her blue bandana. "Those cigarettes are brutal," she groaned.

We continued our approach on foot, ready to jump and hide if anybody came up or down the road. Before we reached the tall basalt columns that served as Thorp's gate posts, we climbed a hillside that would eventually give us a look down onto the buildings.

As we climbed, meadowlarks sang and a few small mule deer bounded away through the sage. A couple of cows in the distance stood frozen, heads up, jaws locked in mid-mastication. We crept further uphill, keeping a brushy mound between us and the compound. Near the top, Twyla gave me a slight nod and we scrambled to a rocky outcrop.

Through binoculars we could see the rear of the ramshackle ranch-style structure that Thorp used as his home and studio. Higher on the lot was a nearly complete log-and-stone edifice. It was massive, the reward, I supposed, of the cryptocurrency scheme. I imagined its walls would soon be hung with hunting trophies, bull elk with impressive antlers and glass eyes that followed you around the room accusingly.

"Nobody outside," whispered Twyla. "Let's get a bit closer."

A cluster of trees provided cover as we dropped toward the older home. I saw motion behind the sliding glass door off the deck—a figure in a red hat—and immediately signaled to Twyla as if we had been doing silent reconnaissance together for years. We turned our binoculars on the window. When I finally managed to focus through the reflection on the big glass door, I recognized Thorp's broadcast studio, the old desk and the recording equipment—and was that Nigel sitting in a chair in front of the desk? It certainly looked like him, and although it was difficult to see deeper into the room, somebody else seemed to be seated behind him.

Twyla, I noted, had traded her Nikon binoculars for the Smith & Wesson pistol she carried. She was looking at me with a barely contained fury, on the verge of bounding down the slope. Wait for the sheriff? Her body language said no way.

I pointed to a nearby vantage point. She sighed, and we moved 50 feet to our right. She pointed to the driveway, which was occupied by Nigel's massive SUV and an orange Camaro. So, it was Nigel in the studio. And Beth was with Nigel today.

Now it was my turn to want to charge down the hill, crash through the glass door, and clobber Thorp with the same rock I'd hoisted on my first visit to his studio.

But Twyla's free hand was on my chest, holding me back. She pointed with the gun to a back room, where a casement window was cranked open. Twyla began creeping down the hill, stopping every third or fourth step like a cat stalking a bird. I followed on less cat-like joints.

Once we reached the back wall of the house, we monkey-crawled toward a faucet located directly below the open window. We pulled ourselves to sitting positions on either side of the dripping hose bib, our backs to the wall, and listened to the muffled voices inside. A few fat raindrops splattered on our knees. I felt heavier rain drops, and then a sudden warmth and wetness spread all over my right ear. Had a gutter overflowed above me? Was I bleeding? Then I felt the cold nose and heard the snuffling. Penny's golden front end was hanging out of the window. She was excitedly nuzzling and licking at my head.

"Get the hell back here, you runt." Boots scraped and somebody yanked Penny's leash, pulling her abruptly back through the window. She yelped and I heard her whining.

"Shut up, dog." Penny whimpered as the scraping boots led her away. I'd heard that voice before.

Twyla waited a few minutes, then, with a quick nod to me, she was through the window before I could push myself off the ground to follow. I scrambled to join her, and once inside what seemed to be a bedroom, we heard muffled voices from the other side of the house. More angry words, then a loud, sharp blast.

Thunder? Some kind of explosion in the studio?

Or a gunshot?

Before I could come to a conclusion, lightning lit the room and another eardrum-shattering crack shook the house. In the studio down the hall, Penny howled, then began a furious growling. A voice —loud, disgusted, dismissive—came from the studio, its owner complaining about a "cheap-ass fire" and a cigarette. I heard Twyla take a deep breath as she adjusted her grip on her gun, grasping it in both hands and holding it near her chest. We exchanged a brief look, then charged toward the studio.

As we burst into the room, our gazes trained over the barrel of Twyla's gun, another flash blazed, lighting the scene before us. For an instant I was blinded and I felt the explosion of thunder through the floorboards more than I heard it. But I'd seen what I feared I might: Beth, cowering on a spindly chair, her wide open eyes telegraphing her terror.

I pushed Twyla aside and darted through the studio's doorway just as a high-pitched scream drowned the sound of the storm. There, for the second time in my life, I experienced the profoundly unsettling certainty that I stood face-to-face with an alternate vision of myself. Bright orange and pulsating, he wore my red Queen Anne baseball hat and a curiously exhilarated expression, like an early Renaissance painting of some minor saint encircled by a halo of flames.

Chapter 17

Beth comes close to completely

losing her sh— cool

I was sorriest about the girl, only 16 years old and the pride of her family. She'd had a life ahead of her until now. Maybe rodeo queen, then high school valedictorian, then—to her father's everlasting joy —an engineer. Or an attorney.

But, let's be honest, I was also pretty sorry about me. To die in a dingy hole like this one, trussed up to Nigel? It seemed positively medieval.

Not that I planned on going quietly. I breathed three counts in and four counts out, trying to slow my galloping heart and assess our options.

Thorp and The Doppelgänger had marched us through the little house to a shoebox-shaped bedroom that seemed to be serving as the recording studio for the Voice of Colockum Ridge. Two cylindrical microphones stood upright on the battered wooden teacher's desk that took up most of the room. A pair of black, over-the-ear headphones connected to each of the mics, and behind these recording stations sat a moderately-sized computer monitor, a set of speakers, and two halo lamps with pink bulbs. The floor was carpeted in mismatched pieces of deep pile, and chunks of foam sound insulation covered the walls, except for the spot taken by an aluminum-framed sliding glass door. It gave out to a view of the detritus of rural life: two dented kettle barbecues among a forest of sun-bleached plastic patio chairs, a set of balding tires, various lengths and widths of lumber and pieces of wire. In the distance, I could see a new home under construction.

Nigel and I were bound to two wooden kitchen chairs placed back-to-back a couple of feet in front of the desk. While The Doppelgänger held his rifle on us, Thorp yanked our arms behind us and tied our hands together as well as to the chairs, the way victims are always tied in heist movies. I'd seen this so many times that our position seemed familiar to me, like maybe I'd been here before and had gotten out alive. Somehow that was a confidence boost, even if it wasn't true. Count it as an advantage.

Also a plus: To bind us, Thorp used the cheap, yellow plastic rope you often see in tangled coils by the side of the highway, sometimes alongside whatever it had failed to hold inside a truck bed. Even now it felt slippery on my sweating hands.

Advantage number three: Thorp tied our hands and arms together around the back of the chairs, and he bound both of us at the ankles. But he neglected to rope our legs to the chairs or to each other. I flexed my ankles, trying to see if I could get my feet flat on the floor. I could.

Lindsey had been placed next to Nigel and me. She slumped moodily on an ancient metal folding chair that sat beside a heavy, round card table—a beat-up ringer for the 1930s version I'd inherited from my grandparents. Made to last, that thing weighed a ton. On top of the table sat a tangle of HDMI cables, a torn carton of cigarettes with several packs missing, a lighter, and a gallon-sized glass jar filled with hard candies in the shape of root beer barrels.

As we'd entered the house, I had dropped Penny's leash and she'd skittered away on her long nails. I allowed myself to hope that she'd escaped somehow, but as the night receded and a stormy morning dawned, The Doppelgänger dragged her into the room. He looped Penny's leash around a leg of the card table, and there she sat, snarling and snapping, next to a bag of charcoal briquettes and a can of lighter fluid.

Anyone could see The Doppelgänger hadn't bothered to bind Lindsey or adequately secure Penny. He must have figured a spoiled dog and skinny girl weren't much of a threat to him, and this, I figured, might be our biggest edge against him.

And then there was Thorp.

After he tied us up, The Voice of Colockum Ridge took a couple of steps toward The Doppelgänger and dusted his hands one against the other as if to say, "Now there's a job well done!" The Doppelgänger, though, was unimpressed.

"You don't care about this county or this country," he said in a low, poisonous voice. "You care about Roger Thorp, and how he can get a bigger audience. Be the next Dexter Carson, right? As if you're a good enough man for that, you goddamn traitor."

"Hold on now," Thorp began, but The Doppelgänger silenced him by placing the muzzle of his rifle to Thorp's lips.

"You want to explain?" he said. "Let's have you explain, then." He moved behind Thorp and gave him a hard shove toward the desk. The older man stumbled forward, then collapsed into a chair behind one of the microphones. The Doppelgänger sat down at the second station and placed one set of headphones on Thorp and the other set on his own head. "Roger," he said, his thin lips curling into a smile. "Time for your show."

"We can't just go live," Thorp said. "This isn't our time slot."

"Don't be stupid, Roger. The Voice of Colockum Ridge can do anything he wants." The Doppelgänger snickered and tapped a few computer keys. "We can livestream on your channel anytime, and Matty's already waiting for us. You're there, right, Matty?"

A chuckle came through the computer's speakers. "Sure, I am—nothing else to do at sunrise. Your camera's not on, though, boys. You want to get that?"

"Nah, no videocast this time," said The Doppelgänger. "Just going to do a short special edition for a select audience." He poked Thorp in the ribs with his rifle. "Right, Roger?"

Thorp didn't answer.

"You all right there, Roger?" asked Matty as The Doppelgänger adjusted his rifle so that it tapped Thorp's temple.

"Yeah," Thorp managed. "Let's go."

"Live from the land of the patriots," Matty began, "it's a special wildfire edition of Straight Talk. And here he is, the Voice of Colockum Ridge, Roooo-ger Thorp!"

"Good morning, everyone," Thorp began. "We're here kind of unexpectedly this morning." He faltered, and looked questioningly at The Doppelgänger.

"Because we're going to get at the truth behind all these fires you started, Roger," The Doppelgänger said smoothly. I felt Nigel tense behind me.

"You mean, all the fires you started," Thorp said. "Folks, we got our upper county arsonist here live—"

The Doppelgänger yanked the plug out of Thorp's microphone.

"Hey, what's going on, you guys?" Matty's uncertain voice came through the computer speakers again. "We lost Roger's mic."

"When you follow the money, Roger," The Doppelgänger said into his mic, "it all leads right back to you. And I can explain that. I can explain all of 'em."

He took a deep breath. "Happy Mountain fire, I'll give you that first since the fire investigators are going to figure it out anyway. It really was just an accident. Roger's little server farm, the one he uses for mining WorkCoin? It got too hot and did some sparking. Oopsy, right, Roger?"

Thorp leaned toward the live mic. "I never," he began. The Doppelgänger tapped the older man's cheek with the rifle and he went quiet.

"Next, the La Likt River fires. The ones the old couple in their van were supposed to have started. You wanted to get back at your snooty neighbors up here on the ridge. So, you had me trick them into going up the river looking for some kind of rare bird. Then all I had to do was drop a few lit briquettes in the grass behind their rig. Make it look like they were dragging a chain. That was my idea."

He laughed and said in a rush, "Of course, that went so well, we figured why not light up Rocky Ridge and make it look like The Peckerwood did it? You can't stand The Peckerwood, or his nosy wife. Don't like the people in Skylandia much, either, do we? All of those wonks and wokes, looking down on the people who have lived here all of their lives." He glanced over at Nigel and me and smirked, then grabbed Thorp's collar and pulled him across the desk toward the live mic.

"What've you got to say to the audience now, Roger?"

"I didn't set those fires," Thorp croaked. "You set those fires."

The Doppelgänger paused, as if to give his audience a moment to savor the drama. "Well, you're right. It takes somebody with brains and skill to set blazes like that and get away with it."

The thin wail of a distant siren interrupted The Doppelgänger, who cocked an ear toward the studio's open door.

"Well," he said as the sirens sounded louder. "More rigs. Seems like maybe there's another fire, and seems like it might be up our way this time." He laughed. "I'd say you started this one too, Roger, but no one's going to believe that you could do it. People might believe you'd pay a man with the skills to set fires for you. Only, you never did pay me, did you?"

"You'll get paid," Thorp said.

"I'm done waiting around for WorkCoin, Roger. Just imagine what I could've accomplished with that money if I'd had it in time."

He gazed at Thorp and sighed. "Fleets of fire-breathing drones flying across the west. Targeted fires. Unstoppable in this drought, with all the beetle-killed trees. You build multimillion-dollar estates where they shouldn't be and fire shall have dominion. That's what The Peckerwood used to talk about, but he's like you, Roger. Doesn't have the balls to do anything himself."

Sirens screamed in the distance, and The Doppelgänger gave up a choked laugh, like a drowning man going under. "And taking action is how you make things change," he said. "It's how you wake up the human race. Put the brakes on things. Stop the growth and mindless consumption. Maybe even bring about the end times." He pushed Thorp away from the microphone, and the older man stood and took a few shaky steps around the desk toward Nigel and me.

"We could have done big things," The Doppelgänger shouted, getting up from his chair to follow Thorp. "But, shit, that couldn't happen. Because you were never going to pay me anyway, were you?"

"I was," Thorp said, his voice trembling. "I am! After the I.C.O."

The Doppelgänger snorted. "Give me airtime then, too?"

"'Course I will," said Thorp.

"You give the woodpecker piece of shit airtime." The Doppelgänger gestured with the muzzle of his gun toward Nigel. "Then you try to sweet-talk this equally shitty piece of shit into giving you an interview. Like it would be a privilege or something to talk to him when I'm the one who's out here making a real difference."

"I was trying to get them into the house," Thorp began.

The Doppelgänger again snorted, a disgusted "puh!" that seemed to sum up all the disappointments of a life filled with them. Then he raised the rifle, took aim, and casually pulled the trigger.

Thorp's body blew backward past Nigel and me, spattering both of us with blood, bone, and brain. It landed with a hard thump a few feet to my left. I could feel Nigel trembling as I struggled to control my breathing—two in, three out. Next to us, Lindsey sat rigid as a pole even as a clap of thunder boomed so close that the house seemed to jump and shudder. Droplets began to dent the dusty ground outside while the scent of sage and gunpowder filled the room.

An otherworldly sound—high and unwavering—slowly penetrated my ringing ears. Penny emerged from underneath Lindsey's chair—howling once, growling now—her teeth bared. The Doppelgänger turned toward her and aimed his rifle.

"No!" I screamed, feeling Nigel behind me jerk in fear. "Penny, quit it!"

For once, my dog went instantly quiet.

"Huh," The Doppelgänger said, as if impressed. I dropped my head and squeezed my eyes shut, feeling certain he was making his way toward me. But when I opened my eyes expecting to meet his empty gaze, I realized he had moved to the other side of the studio. Now he stood before the sliding glass door, rifle at his side, contemplating the sudden downpour.

"Figures," he said. "This is not going to be good for my ridge fire."

Lindsey's chair gave a slight creak, and wrenching my neck, I caught a glimpse of her sitting forward on the cracked vinyl seat cushion, her back arched. She turned quickly to look at Nigel and me, and I was baffled to see a small, tight smile flash across her lips before she turned her body back toward the mumbling man who held the rifle.

"Now I'm going to have light up the whole house, and how's that going to look," The Doppelgänger shouted in disgust, lecturing the rain. "Like I don't know how to start a fire on a tinder-dry ridge? Like I have to start some cheap-ass fire in a house filled with accelerants?" After a moment, he announced in a loud, flat voice, "No. It's going to have to look like someone else got careless with a cigarette." He turned back to us and smiled tightly. "Fire's going to start with you, Nigel."

Lightning lit the darkened sky outside like a strobe and thunder boomed close behind it as Lindsey sprang from her chair. She held the lighter fluid at arm's length, squeezing the fuel out in a fine spray while she put the lighter to the can's nozzle.

The stream of fire touched The Doppelgänger's chest first, then spread upward. His rifle fell to the floor as he turned and raised his arms to his face. His high-pitched scream, an echo of Penny's howl, showed off the room's acoustics while the smell of barbecuing meat filled the air. Flames licked the foam walls.

"Run!" I yelled at Lindsey. "Get Penny's leash!" A foul black smoke roiled across the ceiling as Nigel and I struggled to our feet and began a crouched hopping toward the front door, Nigel pulling one way as I pulled the other.

"Hop toward the door!" I commanded, trying to shout above The Doppelgänger's screams. He was rolling on the carpet now, coming close to our feet, and then flipping back again. "Hop when I say hop, Nigel!"

"No! Hold still!" Twyla was suddenly on her knees in front of me, working at the melting plastic rope that held my feet together. I struggled to sort out the fact of her presence, willing myself not to kick as she untied the knots. Then, I saw The Doppelgänger emerge from the greasy, black smoke. "Watch out!" I shrieked. "He's going for Nigel!"

I lost my footing as Nigel attempted to turn away from The Doppelgänger, which in our current connected state meant throwing me into the wild man's path. I felt myself lifted off the ground and scrabbled wildly to find the floor.

"Freeze, Nigel!" Twyla yelled. "It's Nathan! He'll untie you!" Finished with my knots, she stood up and started for the door. "Go," she shouted as she pushed me. "Now! Go, go, go!"

Something warm and wet touched my ankle. The form on the ground was unrecognizable now, but his hand—unquestionably human—gripped my foot. On the back of the hand, like a brand on a steer, were the letters "L-A". On the four clenched fingers were the letters, "L-I-K-T."

I screamed and felt myself yanked backward as Nigel, feet unbound, pulled both chairs and me toward the front door. The old wood splintered into kindling as, hands still tied together, Nigel and I burst out of the smoke-filled house and sprawled side by side in the muddy driveway. Lindsey and Penny dropped down beside us. "Nathan!" Twyla shouted in our faces. "Where is he?"

In the doorframe, my husband appeared. Something twiggy, a desiccated version of Nathan himself, hung around his shoulders. He limped into the mud and collapsed under the weight of his load.

Sirens keened in the distance as we watched the house burn.

Chapter 18

Brooklyn throws a party

Everyone crowded into the Drake's backyard for Brooklyn's party. Everyone wore cowboy boots. They all gave thanks for the rain that ended the fires. They all welcomed the sun that shone down just as the party started. There was cake. Everyone drank Dave's beer. Except not Lindsey or Brooklyn or the dogs.

"Holly home now," said the party's hostess, who was sitting in Beth's lap. Her legs stuck straight out from under her blue dress, and she was full of admiration for her own new, size 3½ sky blue and bright white boots.

"Holly's family goes home to the sanctuary tomorrow, Brooklyn," Beth whispered back to the girl, stroking her hair.

"Holly home," insisted the girl, turning her head toward Beth.

"Maybe, Brookie."

"Penny and I could certainly try again," said the angular Brit, standing downwind of Beth and Brooklyn, a cigarette in one hand and a pint glass full of fresh amber ale in the other. "Just a matter of —"

"Yes, Nigel," Beth interrupted, "thinking like a chimp. Let's get everybody home to the sanctuary. Then we'll see."

"Well," Nigel said, head bowed modestly, "I stand ready to do my part. Again."

"Oh for the love of—" Beth began.

Big Red was studiously licking the knee of the girl on Beth's lap.

*****

Penny was sitting directly on top of Nathan's left foot. Leaning into his shin. Eyes half-shut and almost nodding off in the golden sunshine. A pilsner glowed in Nathan's hand.

"I really couldn't talk to you," explained Muriel. "Sorry for being so rude."

"No," said Nathan, taking a sip, "you were just doing your job. I was a suspect, so of course you couldn't buddy around with us as usual."

"Dave was on notice, too," Muriel added, looking over at Dave, Glenn/Ben, and Bill Chaney, who all stood near the grill.

"Did he know about Twyla? Who she was?"

"Oh yeah. No secrets in marriage, right?"

"No secrets," Nathan repeated. "Except—well, anyway, Dave's lips were sealed when it came to me, all right."

"Twyla told me that you were quite entertaining," said Muriel, eyes on Nathan as she lifted her Irish-style stout toward her lips.

"She's good at her job."

Muriel licked the foam off her upper lip and asked, "Do you think I could ever go undercover like that?"

"Think you'd like that?" he replied.

"I do."

"Everyone is full of secrets, Muriel. You'd do fine."

Nathan finished his pilsner and moved away to collect a few frosting-smeared plates. As he walked to the kitchen, hands full, he wondered when he'd tell Beth about his meeting with The Doppelgänger on Red Top.

If he would.

*****

Lindsey's little black-and-white dog Emmet had taken a shine to Sheriff Peters. The sheriff seemed to reciprocate those feelings and was crouched down in his off-duty jeans and grey fleece top, giving the little fellow a two-handed rub on the belly and throat.

"Hector," Peters said, his pint of IPA temporarily at ease on the flagstone near his knee, "it looks like Thorp's arsonist won't ever bother your family again."

"Well, even if he recovers from the burns," said Hector, "he'll be in prison for a long time."

"Exactly," said the off-duty lawman.

"Thank God," said Lindsey. "And that SP group he belongs to. Stop Population? I imagine their fundraising will drop off a bit."

"Well," said the sheriff, a little uncertainly, "thank you, Lindsey." The little dog head-butted his knee, requesting even more vigorous attention. "You were brave and smart. And the statements you gave were absolutely perfect. Never heard a more articulate deposition. That must have been hard for you, after everything that happened." He paused, and took a tiny sip of his beer. "None of my business, but do you have someone you're talking to about, you know, what happened?"

"We hope you'll be willing to talk to the investigators about the Happy Mountain fire," the girl quickly replied. "My papa's company can't afford to have those lies hanging out there."

"Course not. Of course I'll be there. And you can be damn sure that little twerp Heath won't be testifying."

"Might need some legal counsel of his own, right?" Lindsey said.

"That's correct," he said, eyeing the young woman. "You're so calm under pressure and you're fast on your feet. I get the feeling you're not interested in law enforcement, but ever think of law school?"

Hector Hernandez turned away and looked up, his eyes suddenly moist, pretending to assess the health of the pines in the Drake's backyard.

*****

"But Nathan told me they can't find the founder. You know, the funder, I mean, of WorkCoin."

Dave the brewer, usually not one to overuse his own products, was into his third beer of the afternoon. Possibly his fourth.

"I'll take over at the tap, sweetie," Twyla said, bumping Dave aside with her hip and taking an empty glass from Bill Chaney, who was standing patiently at the keg station. "Getting pretty good at this."

"Well, they're still working on it," Bill finally answered, now that he could see his beer being pulled by the undercover fire investigator.

"Amazing the paper trail you can find on all that crypto stuff," Twyla said as she coaxed the last of Bill's ale into his perfectly foam-capped glass. "I mean, the whole point of these blockchain set ups is to avoid tracking, right? Secret payments, right? Off-the-books shenanigans. But Thorp's emails spell it all out."

"But if they don't find her," asked Dave. "The founder, I mean. Then who's on the hook for the fire at the Bountiful warehouse?"

"Well," Twyla answered, tugging a brew for Nathan, who had sidled up to the keg zone. "The Italian and Mr. Electric are cooperating. They might get off with a slap. Thorp is still on a slab in Ellensburg and I don't think he's hopping off it anytime soon."

"Seems like Dr. LaVonne Heath might be left holding the bag," Bill Chaney opined with evident satisfaction. In fact, the lawyer let a broad smile grow across his handsome face as the pint glass returned for another visit.

"Do tell," said Dave, looking from tap-girl Twyla to smiling Bill, then back again.

"Well," Twyla said, "Dr. Heath stage-directed the coverup at the Bountiful warehouse, he tried to frame Hector, and he conveniently removed and/or planted evidence related to the La Likt River fires and the Rocky Ridge fire."

"That enough for you?" she added as she curled the foam top on Nathan's pilsner as if it was a golden cappuccino.

"What a conceited chump," said Nathan, accepting the beer from his femme fatale.

"And get this," said Bill, leaning forward. "His degree from Stanford? Turns out he took one summer workshop on fire investigation taught by a Stanford assistant professor. At a community college."

"To the late Dr. Heath," said Dave, raising his glass in toast.

Roxy the chihuahua was suddenly at the feet of the keg-centric group, directly below Dave's hoisted beer glass, and yapping so hard that her short legs were spending more time off the ground than on it.

"May he rest in prison," finished Bill, his glass raised to join Dave's and Nathan's but his eyes distracted, scanning the backyard for his wife, who was never far from Roxy.

*****

"Take her for a while," said Beth. "She's getting sleepy."

James Novak had spent most of the afternoon lounging in an Adirondack chair in the far corner of the Drake's backyard. His huge blue down jacket served as both butt-pad and backrest and he had found one of Penny's old pillows to use as a headrest. Other than keeping a distant eye on his daughter, his main preoccupations during Brooklyn's party had been napping, sipping from a tall insulated cup of tea, and reading from Nathan's thick climate report.

"Hello, Brookie," he said, taking his daughter from Beth and letting her fall into his lap. He tugged on his blue jacket to create a partial cover for her. The sun breaks were ending and a late afternoon cloud cover was building.

"Thank you, Beth," he said.

"You'll come up to the sanctuary with us tomorrow? It's a big day and I know Brooklyn wants to be there."

"Yeah. Of course."

"I'm so glad you're here," said Beth. "It'll be great to have you nearby, working at the sanctuary."

Penny sidled up to Beth and poked a cold nose into her hand.

The clouds piled against the western horizon shifted slightly, allowing a flat beam of golden light to escape down the full length of the upper Sahaptin Valley, accentuating the deep cedar grain of the Drake's cabin and causing all the greens and browns of the backyard to suddenly vibrate and sharpen.

"You know," James said, cradling his daughter, "my mother asked me once who might be the best guardian for Brookie. If Chloe and I, you know, were out of the picture."

Beth didn't respond.

"You were the one," he continued, "the one we all wanted. My mom loved you so much. Working with you. She was so glad when you and Nathan moved up here. Especially after Dad died."

"I loved her very much," Beth managed to say.

Penny stood nearby, her brow of golden furrows aimed at Beth.

*****

"How are you doing?" Nathan asked.

"I'm okay," sighed Beth. "Life goes on."

The guests had departed at sunset. James was inside reading to Brooklyn before bedtime. Nathan stood behind Beth and wrapped his arms around her as they watched the remnants of a cloud-muted sunset.

"Ready for the big move tomorrow?" Nathan asked.

"I am. I don't know if they are."

On cue, a couple chimps exchanged soft hoots in the garage.

"It'll be nice to have our garage back," Nathan said.

"Will you miss them at all?" Beth asked.

"You'd think I'd be fascinated by the proximity to our closest relatives in the animal world."

"You'd think, Mr. Scientist."

"But frankly, they creep me out," he said. "I go in there, and it's like they're so similar. But also completely different. A total mystery."

"Kind of like other people, right?"

"Yeah, welcome to the human race, I guess."

"This afternoon was nice, don't you think?"

"I enjoyed the party. At least you know what friends are thinking, most of the time."

"Yeah, the whole speaking-thoughts-aloud thing helps too, right?"

"Right."

"So, no more plans for the monastery in Santa Barbara?"

"We'll have our hands full for a while."

"From big chimps, plural to little monkey, singular."

"I'm looking forward to the time with Brooklyn. Lots to learn."

"Like when we took in Penny. Sort of."

"James should finish his program next month. He might be eligible to take her after that."

"He might need our help, and Cassie's, for a while."

"He's on the right track."

"Let's hope Chloe follows."

"One step at a time."

They heard James from somewhere inside the cabin adopting the voice of a silly bear as he read to Brooklyn. They heard Brooklyn laugh and laugh and laugh. The bear voice got even sillier.

"Beth, do you think we'll need more space?"

"What? Like a room off the new garage?"

"Or something different"

"Something different?"

"Like those new places above town. Bill and Kathy said they were really nice. Huge kitchens."

"You want a house?"

"One of those places would also have room for the horse Paula was boarding down in Ellensburg."

"You want a horse?"

"Just thinking. Brooklyn might like that someday."

"A lot to think about, honey."

"One step at a time. You're right."

"Go in?"

Returning up the front path, hand in hand, they saw Penny in the soft light of the living room, chin resting on the back of the sofa, monitoring their slow progress toward the door.

Epilogue

Sanctuary regained

The rain, when it finally comes, surprises her. It falls in stinging beads against her skin and turns the blackened ground beneath her feet into an ashy paste that sticks. She cradles her cowboy boot in both arms and leans back into the rust-colored snag at the top of the pasture—all that was left of her favorite Ponderosa pine.

Once Red and Brooklyn were gone, she had made her way back over the ridges and through the creek beds to this hillside above the pasture that was once her home. The trip back had taken much longer than their frantic escape on the first night of the fire. The landscape, after all, was radically different. Seemingly random patches of forest still rich with huckleberry, pine, and bright red mountain ash gave way to miles of charred trees, sharp rocks, and smoking stumps. Holly would start off in one direction only to find, upon topping a ridge, that the view before her was more patchwork green and rusty gray, not the familiar outbuildings and pastures of Cassie's place. But once she had passed under the power lines, she knew the way.

The rain gives way to a fine mist. Below her, Holly sees a vehicle pull into the muddy driveway that leads to Cassie's house. Two dogs and four people pop out as if they'd been packed inside under pressure. One of the people—a woman, Holly judges—holds a child. The woman bends at the waist and sets the small one on her feet, then takes the child's hand in her own.

Brooklyn. Holly leans forward and hoots. The people in the yard look up at her pasture, and the dogs start toward her before being called back. "Penny, come!" she hears one of the people yell. "Red Boy, here!"

Holly shrinks back against the ruined tree. After a moment, the two men—Holly judges them to be male by their size—walk toward the chimp house. The woman and little one follow behind more slowly.

All morning, Holly watches as the people drag her possessions out of the chimp house. The mattresses she and her community used for sleeping, the aluminum buckets that held fruit, grains, water, and sometimes, for a treat, Kool-Aid. Deflated balls. Chalkboards. Mangled stuffed animals. She hoots when she sees those, too, but this time only Brooklyn looks up toward the hillside.

From her perch, she hears snippets of conversation. "James, where did Cassie say she put the buckets?" and "Think this is worth salvaging, Beth?" At lunchtime, the group sits around the back of their open car, eating sandwiches.

Holly's stomach burns. She hasn't eaten much since she left the abundance of the townhome. There wasn't a lot to eat left in the forest, and besides, she'd never lived in the wild. She was used to having her meals delivered. And this was her favorite time of year— lots of melons, tomatoes, and sweet corn.

After lunch, the people below finish sorting the contents of the chimp house into two sodden heaps near the spot where the big shed once stood. They take up three of the least damaged buckets, rinse them, and fetch new brooms and mops from the back of their car. A familiar, slightly tinny sound drifts from the chimp house on the stiff breeze. A male voice, a crowd cheering. Baseball, Holly signs, though Cassie isn't there to see her.

Twice she starts down the hill and through the pasture toward the chimp house. Brooklyn is there, she knows, and Red. A plate filled with corn. A new mattress. Twice she turns and scampers back up to the burned tree. If she gives up what she has now, she senses she'd never get it back.

The mist burns off and the sun comes out, heating the scorched ground around her until she feels the dampness rise in steamy waves. She falls asleep, awakes, and sleeps again until a sound from the yard below teases her awake.

Cassie's truck comes up the drive, pulling the chimp trailer. The door to the truck's cab opens, and Cassie gets out and walks into the chimp house. In their trailer, the chimpanzees drum on the metal floor and call out to one another.

Holly shifts forward onto her knuckles and watches as Cassie leads the people, laden with buckets and mops, from the chimp house. They gather in a group slightly up the hill, behind the ruins of the shed. Cassie goes to the trailer, unlocks the door, and leads Freddy Chimpanzee into the house.

One after the other, the chimps return home as Holly watches. When all six are inside, Cassie closes the door and motions for her friends to come down from the hill.

Cradling her cowboy boot, Holly hesitates one final time, savoring this odd pleasure—a new feeling, maybe Cassie will teach her a sign for it—this moment between the adventure ending and her familiar life beginning again.

The End

ACKNOWLEDGMENTS

Many thanks to:

- Dan Courter (1951-2023), first and best reader and brother extraordinaire. You are always in our hearts.

- Greg Hollobaugh, designer of elegant, eye-catching covers for Penny. So lucky to have you for a friend and contributor.

- Phil Welch, film editor and screenwriter, who is finding Penny a home in Hollywood.